THE OLD MAN OF THE STARS

Borgo Press Books by JOHN BURKE

The Golden Horns: A Mystery Novel
Murder, Mystery, and Magic: Macabre Stories
The Old Man of the Stars: Two Classic Science Fiction Tales

THE OLD MAN OF THE STARS

TWO CLASSIC SCIENCE FICTION TALES

JOHN BURKE

THE BORGO PRESS

MMXI

THE OLD MAN OF THE STARS

FIRST EDITION

Published by Wildside Press LLC

www.wildsidebooks.com

THE OLD MAN
OF THE STARS

CONTENTS

ACKNOWLEDGMENTS

These stories were previously published in magazine form as follows, and are reprinted by permission of the author:

"The Old Man of the Stars" was first published in *Authentic Science Fiction*, September 1953. Copyright © 1953, 2011 by John Burke.

"The Recusants" was first published in *Authentic Science Fiction*, February 1957. Copyright © 1957, 2011 by John Burke.

THE OLD MAN
OF THE STARS

CHAPTER ONE

In the green twilight, warm with the promise of the long Elysian summer, the young men and women were strolling and talking below the white steps of the Community Palace. The pliant trees murmured in the faintest of breezes, and the planet's two moons were rising above the distant hills.

The old man on the terrace sat with his eyes half-closed and thought about home—about Earth.

He did not look old. He had the smooth, handsome face of a young man of twenty-five, and there was no grey in his hair. There was something almost youthfully arrogant about his lean features and jutting chin. Only in his eyes was there the weariness of age. Brooding over the scene before him, he was conscious of the heavy weight of centuries on his shoulders. A great time and a great space separated him from the world of his birth.

A young woman walked slowly past him. She wore the loose, casual tunic and shorts that were customary during the leisure hours on Elysium: and most hours on this tranquil planet were leisure hours.

The old man reached out and caught hold of her golden-brown arm for a moment. She stopped, with a slight grimace of distaste.

He said: "This evening it is just like it was in the old world."

"Indeed, Matthew?" she said politely.

"But of course we didn't get this green light. The glow of sunset was something that nobody here but myself remembers. You've never known anything like it."

"No, I'm afraid we haven't."

He was aware of the scent of her fresh young body; and aware also of the restraint and pity behind her politeness. Pity? There were times when he was sure it verged on contempt. Contempt...for him, the oldest and wisest of them all, who had been on this planet for centuries before any of them had existed!

He let go of her arm. A young man hurried up beside her. They exchanged smiles, nodded briefly to Matthew, and walked away.

"A romantic evening, isn't it?" he called after them, but they did not reply. Perhaps they had not heard him. Or perhaps, like so many of their contemporaries, they could no longer be bothered with him.

Matthew sighed. They were bored by his reminiscences, and the young woman shrank from his touch. However young he might remain in appearance, he was too old.

He looked up into the heavens, where the stars seemed brighter and more magnificent than they had ever seemed on Earth. But at least on Earth they had been regarded as a challenge. Men had stared up and vowed to reach those distant worlds: they had launched themselves into space, braving its hazards and accepting the demands their explorations made on them. Men had been ambitious then.

Here on Elysium the challenge was ignored. Across the generations ambition had died. This was a planet of warmth and contentment, and today there were few who wished to reach any further.

There were even fewer who were interested in the prospects of a return journey that they would not live to finish. Only a handful of social misfits listened to Matthew's pleas.

Thinking of his vain plans, he noticed Raymond in the distance, and beckoned him over. Raymond was a tall, middle-aged man with dark features, creased by lines of impatience. He walked with an aggressive briskness that was uncommon on this world. His gestures were curt and decisive. When he reached Matthew, he gave him a sort of mock salute and stood looking down at the older man with an air of exasperation that meant nothing—it was the expression he always wore.

Matthew said: "How are things going? I haven't been over for a day or two."

"I know that," was the brusque response. "And you won't find much change when you do come."

"That hold-up over materials was settled, though, wasn't it?"

"After a fashion. But it's never really been a question of materials. Elysium is rich enough in mineral wealth. It's the men themselves. They're losing interest again."

Matthew began to push himself up from his chair, then slumped back again. He said:

"But that new group seemed quite keen at first."

"They always do," said Raymond sardonically, "at first. Then they began to feel there's no point in the whole thing; They start asking questions about why we want to send a ship back to Earth, and what good it will do anybody."

"But that has all been explained and given official sanction by the Community Delegates."

Raymond shrugged. "It's being said that the Delegates only do it to humour you."

"To humour me?"

"Of all the men and women who would come with you on the voyage," said Raymond, "you would be the only one to reach the destination."

"We've gone into all that before."

"And quite apart from that," the other went on, "there's a very strong body of opinion that holds there isn't any destination. There are experts who say that Earth is only a myth—a myth you've talked yourself into believing.

Matthew gave vent to a wild splutter of indignation. The presumptuousness of these idlers, these lotus-eaters, was becoming quite fantastic.

And yet he had had ample warning of this tendency in recent times. In the past, long ago, he had been respected by historians and scholars. They had come to him to check their facts. He had actually lived through the past ages, and was therefore a source of first-hand information. He could verify things, explain details that baffled the historians. Once or twice, though, they had caught him out in trivial errors. No one man could know everything that had happened at any given time, even if he had been alive then; but these mistakes made one or two experts say that Matthew was not reliable. He was accused of inventing things. His stories of the conquest of the far reaches of space, which had once been regarded as accurate history, came to be viewed with reserve. Gradually it was murmured that he was a maker of fables rather than a reliable chronicler. His reminiscences of life on Earth took on the character of a mythology. Historians who had worked along certain theories and then had them denied by Matthew, openly stated that Matthew was wrong. If he verified their findings, they quoted him. If he contradicted them, they shook their heads and said that he didn't know what he was talking about. They were men of great learning, and who was this relic of the past that he should dare to question their knowledge?

There came the time when few referred to Matthew at all. They said his memory wandered. They said he was at best inaccurate and feeble-minded, and at worst a teller of tall stories.

But it was not true. Matthew remembered all right:

clearly and nostalgically across the centuries, he remembered everything.

* * * * * * *

He remembered his friend Philipson, a biologist at a time when physicists were the great lords of the scientific world. Philipson professed to have no great interest in the conquest of space, but he pointed out one of the major problems that would confront the explorers when the time came.

"It's all right to talk of new power drives that will send a ship to our neighbouring planets in a matter of months," he said many times to Matthew; "even at the greatest speed that may be achieved in that way, how long is it going to take to reach the stars? Men will die of old age before they get there. The ships may survive—it may even be possible to develop fuel that will carry them on across the years—but there won't be anyone left on board to pilot them."

And when he had said that, he would chuckle and prophesy that one fine day even the interplanetary and interstellar flight technicians would be acknowledging the importance of a biologist's work.

Philipson was working on the prolongation of human life. In moments of great enthusiasm, carried away by his obsession, he would declare that the secrets of immortality were within his grasp.

Matthew was several years younger than his friend. He was not a scientist. His interests lay in other directions. He looked forward to a career in the

Interplanetary Development Corporation—a financial career. Already his father's firm of brokers was expanding as the first stages of Martian colonisation and development took place. There were setbacks— a series of disasters to some of the early space ships, for example—but this was a time when a man with influence in the City used that influence to get his sons or relatives into the I.D.C. Matthew's father had such influence, and Matthew had a head for figures.

"This is going to be something big," said his father. "We won't live to see the really colossal profits that will come as the I.D.C. spreads wider and wider, but at least we'll be comfortable, and more than comfortable, for the rest of our lives."

We won't live to see the really colossal profits.... Comfortable for the rest of our lives....

The words echoed in Matthew's mind. He could not help feeling a certain nagging resentment. He would be one of those who laid the foundations for a future generation that would reap huge profits. Life was too short. He wanted to live a long way into the future: he was ambitious, and he wanted time to get to the top, time to watch men going out to the stars, time to indulge in the pleasures that power and riches might bring.

If only that crank Philipson could strike lucky, and add a couple of hundred years to his life span! Never mind about immortality, a dream with many of the disturbing implications of a dream: two hundred years would do to be going on with.

But although he saw Philipson regularly and listened to his wilder theories over a period of three years in his early twenties, Matthew did not really pay a great deal of attention to what was said. He did not really believe in the possibility of any substantial extension of human life. Ever since the grafting and rejuvenation experiments of the mid-century, there had been steady progress in combatting the worst manifestations of old ages, but a man who lived to be more than a hundred was still a rarity. Senility was less obvious than it had once been, but death was not to be held back.

And then there came that day when, as though for the first time, Matthew took a long look at his friend Philipson and said:

"You're looking very well. You look as though you've been on a long holiday or something."

The other flushed. "Hard work, not holidays," he said with a nervous laugh, and went on to chatter about some recent research in genetics that had attracted his attention.

Matthew did not listen. He studied the brightness of Philipson's restless eyes, and his clear skin. The unhealthy pallor that had once been there was gone. Philipson did not appear to have aged at all in the last year or two. He might have been the same age as Matthew himself. Matthew was, he realized with shock and dawning suspicion, catching up with Philipson.

He suddenly interrupted the flow of technical jargon. He said harshly:

"Philipson, you've found what you were after."

"Mm?" The off-handed reply was unconvincing.

"I believe you've found a serum—a process—something—that will give you immortality."

"Oh, nothing like immortality," Philipson rashly blurted out.

"Then a prolongation of life, at least. A renewal. That's it, isn't it?" Matthew demanded.

"My experiments have had a certain amount of success. But it's early. It's too soon to say. I mean...."

"You mean that you're pretty certain you've done it, and in fact you're confident enough to experiment on yourself."

"Got to use some sort of guinea-pig," said Philipson uneasily.

"Why not me?"

The two men stared at one another. Philipson backed away, resting his right hand on a drawer in a bench and tugging it slightly open.

Matthew went on remorselessly: "Why haven't you published your results? Why are you keeping it all to yourself? You want to live on while others die: you want to take advantage of the rest of the human race."

Philipson shook his head. "You don't understand."

"You'd better try to make me understand then."

There was a long silence. A strange feeling of fear and apprehension seemed to enter into the untidy laboratory.

Matthew was suddenly possessed by the conviction that he had only to reach out and grasp a hundred years, two hundred years of the future: they were within reach, and he was not going to be cheated of them.

At last Philipson said: "There is not yet room enough in the universe. Already Earth is overcrowded, and although Mars is admirably suited to industrial development and can supply Earth with needed raw materials, it will not provide a home for ordinary people. With the conquest of disease the growth of population has been more rapid than ever before, and there has been no major war for thirty years. Unless we can find homes on the other planets for our people—and at present there is no indication that we shall be able to adapt ourselves very easily to the inimical conditions on most of the other planets in this solar system—we are going to face famine in a very short time. Yet you think, knowing all this, that I ought to try to prolong the life of every other human being? If the birth rate stays the same, can't you imagine what the situation will be like? Instead of dying off and making at least a little room for the newcomers, old people will go on living. They won't grow old. The Earth will never sustain them all."

He spoke with conviction. But for Matthew it was not good enough. It might be true that the world would soon be overcrowded if human life were prolonged. But that didn't mean that he, Matthew, was prepared to give up his longing for the future. He said:

"What do you propose to do, then? You can't keep it to yourself."

"My idea is that a small group of brilliant men and women might take advantage of the discovery, without letting the rest of the world know at first. Think of the advantages to everyone else! A man who can afford to spend a hundred years on, say, one piece of research, is going to be able to extend immeasurably the frontiers of knowledge. And in due course, when men have perfected a ship that will reach out to the other star systems, injections can be given to volunteers who will go along with that ship. The journey may take hundreds of years—but they will be alive at the end of it. And somewhere in all the galaxies must be many more planets on which the men of our race can be comfortable. When they have been discovered, longevity can be granted to everybody. Until then, it is best kept secret, shared by a few chosen beings only."

"And did you propose," asked Matthew shakily, "to include me in your choice?"

Philipson hesitated, then said: "No."

"As an old friend, I should have thought—"

"We are friends," Philipson said, "but that doesn't mean I'm blind to your defects, Matthew. You are one of those who search for personal power. I think you might be dangerous. A man who lives beyond the normal span has too much time in which to work mischief. An undying dictator—even an undying financial juggler, holding the economic fate of millions in his hands—is a menace to the future of the race."

Matthew said: "I intend to share in this experiment. You've no right to deny me this gift. After all the encouragement I've given you—"

"It's no use trying to threaten me," cried Philipson.

Matthew advanced towards him. Philipson leaned back against the bench, tugged at the drawer, and drew out a small electronic revolver. It sat in his hand like a little, gleaming cigarette lighter.

Matthew stopped.

"How much would you want?" he asked.

"The secret is not for sale."

"I'm not asking for any secrets. Just give me an injection, or whatever it is. Immortality—"

"Not immortality," snapped Philipson with childish irritation. "An extension of life, yes, but not immortality: not under the conditions that exist on Earth, anyway."

"You mean that somewhere else—perhaps in a different atmosphere, on a different planet...?"

Philipson, once more regarding Matthew as the audience in whom he had so often confided, could not resist going on. He said:

"At the beginning of the twentieth century it was already surmised that there was a connection between the duration of life and the speed of intestinal putrefaction. The simpler theorists just advocated special diets, and every faddist in the world added his own pet idea. But basically the idea is obviously sound. Provided the conditions proper to it are maintained, there's no reason why a living organism should not continue to live. Short of violent death or the onset of disease, every being is potentially immortal. But life is a matter of constant friction. The tissues wear away...but given optimum conditions, they renew themselves. The mid-century experiments in longevity revolved around the possibility of grafting tissue from such creatures as lizards, but they were only temporary expedients. I have always worked on the assumption that the problem would have to be tackled from inside—literally inside the human body.

"Metchnikoff made great play with the theory that the bacteria of putrefaction should be suppressed by another set of microbes. Complete sterilisation is not possible—in fact, it would mean eventual death. The body needs certain bacilli. I have been working all these years on the preparation of cultures that will fight against all the influences of putrefaction and at the same time carry on a steady renewal of the frailer human tissues."

Matthew said: "And you've succeeded, haven't you?"

"I believe so. But the atmosphere of our planet is a strongly destructive force. You know how coastlines are eroded: you've seen how wood can be rubbed away with sandpaper. The human frame is like that: quite apart from the sharper action of bacteria and disease, there is the constant erosion and weakening caused by the mere act of living and breathing. My discovery will prolong life: but I believe we may one day find planets on which the optimum conditions prevail. There will be none of this physical friction. On such a planet, a man who had been injected with this culture might be almost immortal. Only if he came back to Earth would he once more start—though slowly—to wear away."

And as his hand relaxed, letting the electronic revolver

sag, Matthew struck at him suddenly, knocking him sideways. When he recovered his balance, Matthew was holding the gun.

Matthew said: "Now. Come on. I'm not asking much. I just want to take part in your experiment. You can regard me as guinea-pig. I'm willing to take a chance."

Philipson had turned pale. He tried to stammer an appeal, but Matthew was prepared to waste no more time. He barked a peremptory command, and in another minute Philipson was filling a long hypodermic from a small grey culture bottle.

"And no funny business," said Matthew.

Philipson shook his head sadly. He looked at the syringe that he had just laid gently on the bench, and then at Matthew.

"No," he said with sudden violence. "You are not worth it. You're not."

And he jumped.

They crashed against the bench. There was a tinkle of glass and a pungent smell.

Matthew struck Philipson on the side of the head and sent him reeling. Philipson came back with a furious attack that took Matthew's breath away. He hadn't realised the man had it in him.

But Philipson was wasting his breath; shouting, "You're not fit to go on, even as a guinea-pig. I won't let you."

It was not with any deliberately murderous intent that Matthew fired the gun. His hand had closed about it instinctively and suddenly his thumb found the small plunger. Trying to force Philipson away from him, he was conscious of nothing but a blur of anger and the urgency of his need to get hold of that hypodermic, in which lay the seeds of all that the future could hold for him.

He pressed the plunger, and the searing cartridge exploded into white light in Philipson's head. There was a great glow about him, and as he fell backwards a flame licked up ravenously from the end of the bench.

Matthew grabbed the syringe. He plunged the needle into the vein on his left forearm, feeling a strange heat racing up his arm, more agonising than the heat of the flames that raced along the bench and engulfed a whole shelf in a matter of seconds.

He dropped the gun into his pocket and ran for the door.

The laboratory had been transformed into a furnace. Philipson and all the things that Philipson had been working on were utterly consumed. The telecasts that evening paid tribute to a great but little appreciated scientist, and one of the learned societies a month later staged a memorial discussion of various aspects of his work.

Nothing was said about longevity and immortality that wasn't rather mocking. Philipson's main interest had not been taken very seriously by his colleagues. They thought his line of approach had been doomed to frustration.

And Matthew at a later date destroyed the gun, after being congratulated by the police on his narrow escape and thanked for the assistance he had given them in their routine inquiries.

A year or so later, wishing to make still further advances in his social position and also within the Corporation itself, he married the wealthy and beautiful daughter of one of the directors.

* * * * * *

At first it was a successful marriage from the worldly point of view. He and his wife were both selfish, and both acknowledged the fact, so that they struck a working compromise and lived fairly happily together for a time.

For a time: for some years....

Then he noticed that she was looking at him as he had once, speculatively and incredulously, looked at Philipson.

Her face was becoming lined while his remained smooth. She grew middle-aged and shrewish while he stayed young. She began to hate him, her envy turning her speech sour, and she accused him of having affairs with other women. When she became really viciously abusive, he admitted that she was right: he turned on her and scoffed at her fading charms, and boasted of his other conquests. He was still young and vigorous, and by now he was wealthy.

In her anger she did what he ought to have guessed she would do. Her father was dead, but two of her brothers served on the board of directors of the I.D.C., and she went to them with her bitter complaints. They had so far regarded Matthew as being merely a remarkably healthy man who was lucky or intelligent enough to keep in splendid physical condition. "Just what a pack of unobservant men would think!" jeered their sister. Now they studied him, and were staggered by what they saw. They had not realised how many years had gone by since Matthew had married: they had not realised how old he was, and now they faced up to the fact that no man of his age had any natural right to have such a fresh, almost boyish appearance. It was so unnatural as to be frightening.

There were questions. The telecast newsmen got on to the story. Portable cameras whirred in Matthew's face as he came to the I.D.C. translucent perslite tower for a board meeting,

Who was this man who did not grow old? A scared, jealous muttering spread through the city and reached out into the rest of the country. Wild rumours circulated. An immortal man? Even in these enlightened times there were those who could talk fearfully of pacts with the devil.

In the face of the inquiries of his directors and the growing clamour that the telecast scaremongers were whipping up, Matthew lost patience. The truth would have to come out sooner or later. He told it now. He told the truth to his unbelieving, angry directors, and then went on to an interview, which was televised all over the country.

He was called a liar. He was called a freak. He was denounced by public speakers, scientists, and ministers of religion. A fanatic tried to shoot him. Somebody else demanded an investigation into the death of Philipson all those years ago.

But whatever suspicions might attach to the circumstances of Philipson's death, no evidence remained today. Matthew's story remained unshaken. In the original inquiry he had said nothing about the injection he had received, because, he now said, he had not known if it would work

He was Philipson's friend, and had offered to act as Philipson's guinea-pig. At the time he had been sceptical. If he had told the full story at the inquest, he would have been laughed at. Now, however, he knew that Philipson had been right. If only poor Philipson had lived, what a boon he could have bestowed on mankind!

He had always realised that the man in the street would resent the existence of someone else with a long life span, but he had not anticipated quite such jealousy and bitterness as he now had to endure. Life was almost intolerable. Although he was taken up by some of the fashionable hostesses, and asked to give innumerable interviews this phase did not last; only resentment and suspicion were left.

He was forced to resign from the I.D.C. and seek a quieter life in the country. There, boredom crept up on him. The local inhabitants soon discovered who he was, and shunned him or peered at him with dark, superstitious hostility. Occasionally scientists would travel out to see him, trying to sift his memories in the hope that he could give them some clue as to Philipson's work so that they could pursue it and find the answer. But what had he known of the technicalities? Even if he had listened more carefully to Philipson, he would not have understood what he heard.

In the middle of the first interplanetary war with Martian colonists, he tried to join up, giving his age as twenty-five. But he was recognised, and scoffed at. His real age, incredible as it was, was known. It was absurd that any attention should be paid to such a conventional point, when he was obviously fit for service: but it soon came home to him that they did not want him—they did not trust him. He was almost an outcast, thrust away from the rest of the human race.

He considered marrying again at one time, then visualised the same weary process taking place again. His wife would grow old and unattractive and would suffer untold miseries as she saw him remaining young.

Monotony weighed down on him. He had wanted to be a great man, and the world would not let him be one. He was feared. He was a freak. Filled with confused ambitions, he had no outlet for all his energies and forceful impulses.

It was not until he was approaching the end of his second century that escape came.

On that sunny morning in June that he would never forget, a government helicar dropped swiftly from the skies outside his house, and an elderly man in grey uniform came up to the door. He studied Matthew's face with the expression of faint wonderment that everyone wore at such times.

Indoors, he got to the point at once.

"I have come to ask if you are willing to work for us. There is a great challenge in the heavens, and the time has come when we must answer it."

Matthew gazed at him stupidly for a moment. He had sunk into a dull, slumberous existence, and could not respond quickly. He said at length:

"I don't quite get you."

The other man folded his arms. "It is simple enough. We are ready to send out a ship to the stars."

"You mean—"

"I mean that we are going to go beyond the confines of our own solar system. It has taken us a long time to reach this stage. Now we are ready. But there are snags. Serious difficulties, in fact."

Memory stirred. Matthew remembered old conversations old dreams. He said:

"It will take a long time to get there?"

"Several generations will live and die on the ship in the course of the voyage. We have men and women who are prepared to set out in full awareness of that fact. But in addition to them we felt that we should take a chance—we should run the risk of asking you to go also, in the hope that you would survive the whole journey."

There was no hesitation in Matthew's mind. He said: "I'll go."

"It is a great hazard. You may all perish within a very short time. If you do survive, and reach the nearest star systems, none of the people who have set out will ever come home: they will all have died, with the exception of yourself. There is every chance that under such conditions you will all go mad."

"But the attempt has to be made," said Matthew softly. "The stars have been there, waiting for us, for a long time. It's a challenge we can't refuse."

An appreciative smile crossed the other's face. He held out his hand. They shook hands, and as the visitor rose to go he said: "I was doubtful of you when I came here. Now I feel confident. You are one man who must go on this enterprise."

Matthew nodded. "I shall go."

* * * * * * *

And here, after the weary years in space, when children had been born and grown old and died, after adventures on fantastic worlds with generations now dead and forgotten, he was; here he was on Elysium, an old man whose knowledge was regarded as nonsense, whose factual narratives were called fables. An old man in his physical prime but mentally weary, wanting one thing and one thing only—to go home, no matter how long it might take.

CHAPTER TWO

The following day he went to visit the observatory and the construction plant on the far side of the woods.

The buildings were hidden away as though people were ashamed of their very existence. On Elysium the scientist did not hold an honoured place in the community. Research was not frowned on, but it was not encouraged. Only those without the capacity for what the Elysians considered real living—that is, a pleasant pastoral life, making the most of immediate joys—dabbled in the sciences. Living conditions on this planet were ideal. No effort was needed. Work was something you did only to amuse yourself, and there were few who found scientific research amusing. When the world was so idyllic, why struggle and belabour your brain too earnestly?

Matthew walked briskly along the path through the woods. It was a fine morning, but he did not take a great deal of pleasure in it: nearly every morning on Elysium was fine, and where was the charm in that?

As he approached the main road that led down to the massive white building in which lay all his hopes, he noticed a young woman in the shade of the trees above the slope. She did not hear his footsteps. She was looking down wistfully at the entrance to the main workshop.

Matthew said: "What brings you here?"

She started, and gave a little cry. When she turned to face him her eyes widened, but it was with a sort of angry curiosity rather than the distaste he was accustomed to read in the eyes of young women.

"You are old Matthew," she said accusingly.

He grimaced. "Old Matthew," he echoed.

"You are behind the work that is going on down there. You wish to build a ship that will take you back to Earth."

"Yes."

"Why must you do it?" she demanded. "Why? Isn't this world beautiful enough? Life here is sweet."

"For you it is," he said. "You are young."

"But you are not old in any physical sense—you are not tired or ill. Can't you enjoy what life has to offer? Has life here never meant anything to you?"

It was a question he could hardly bring himself to answer. He recalled the joy of those first decades here, when the weary travellers felt that they had at last reached the perfect world. Automatically they had named the planet Elysium. Here they had rested, then set up their homes, gradually building up the small towns and communities, which could exist so easily on the fertile lands all about them. And Matthew had realised that here was a planet that provided what Philipson had called the optimum conditions: here, if anywhere in the universe, was the golden world on which he would be immortal.

Had life here never meant anything to him? It had meant a great deal, at first. And then, as the years rolled by, it had palled. He who had survived the aching, cramped monotony of space and the dangers of galactic exploration now found that contentment was a thing that did not last. He became restless and querulous. A sedentary contemplative life did not suit him.

He looked at the girl's fair complexion and at her mobile, eager mouth. She was all that was young and desirable, seeing life before her as an adventure and a delight. He said:

"I am very conscious of the beauties of this planet. Only someone like myself who has known other worlds can truly appreciate this one."

"Then why must you persist in trying to get back to Earth—if there is such a place?"

"There is indeed such a place," Matthew assured her. "And there are other places that ought to be visited on the way back. When we left Earth, we made many exploratory landings on other worlds. As our numbers grew, and families in the ship increased, we sought out temperate climates and left small colonies there. On at least three worlds we found other races who were friendly, and we left representatives there to work on the construction of spaceships that could return to Earth with the news of what we had found. All across the universe we left groups of Earthmen and their families. Our own ship, overhauled time and time again, went ever onwards...until at last we reached here and sank into this—this slothfulness."

"Not slothfulness," she said: "happiness."

Again she glanced down towards the building below.

Matthew said: "You are concerned about someone?"

"I am worried about your influence on Clifford of the Martin," she said defiantly.

"He's your brother?"

She blushed. "No."

"Oh. I see."

Matthew envied young Clifford. He envied all people who were mortal—all people who were not doomed to go on living as he was, until desire had grown stale and life had lost its savour. Brusquely he said:

"He's one of my most loyal men. He has been on the project from the start. One of the few young men today with a real flair. He's brilliant."

"And you want to take him away, out there." She waved towards the tranquil skies.

"He wants to come," Matthew observed.

"He would be better living out his life here. How can anyone spend a lifetime shut up in a metal box, hurtling through space? That is not—what we were born or."

"Nevertheless," said Matthew, "he wants to come. The spirit of adventure is not yet dead."

"If he goes," she said, "I shall go with him."

Matthew put his hand on her shoulder. She did not flinch, but turned her vexed, appealing face towards him again.

He said: "I hope you will come with us. There will not be many who will volunteer. And now, don't you think you ought to come down and see the ship? Have you ever seen it before?"

"Only when I was a little girl, when it was still regarded as a museum piece, before you started work on it again."

"Then you must certainly come and see the progress we have made."

They went down the slope together and walked along the road below the great bulk of the main workshops.

* * * * * * *

The ship lay in its great cradle, tilted over to one side as the welders crouched over the rocket exhausts and played glaring flames against the metal. The thumping of a machine at the far end of the hall echoed and boomed through the high building.

"This is it," said Matthew: "this is the ship that brought us here—myself and your ancestors. The historians may scoff at most of what I say, and they may claim that there is no such place as Earth, but at least they've never got round to claiming that there was never any space ship. They may have doubts about where it came from, but they can't deny that it's here."

The girl, dwarfed by the enormity of the vessel, looked up at it with an unfathomable expression. Was she trying to imagine herself inside it, flung away from the surface of the only world she had known, out into the vastness of space, in search of an old world that was perhaps only a figment of Matthew's imagination?

He said: "There's Clifford. He must have been in the observatory."

A tall young man in a smooth, one-piece mechanic's plasticoat came hurrying towards them. He looked from Matthew to the girl in surprise.

"Hello, sir. I didn't know you knew Alida."

"We've only just met. I didn't realise you had won a volunteer for us."

Clifford gasped. "I'd no idea...."

"Well, let's leave it for the time being, anyway. We're nowhere near launching day yet, I fancy."

Clifford grimaced. "Men dropping off again. They

don't see the point of working hard. The only comment I've heard in favour of carrying on"—he grinned—"was to the effect that it would be worth getting the job finished so that they could see the back of you, and then everyone would be able to live in peace."

Matthew smiled ruefully.

The two men took Alida up into the interior of the ship. The gangways and floors were all tilted to one side at present, but it was still possible to examine the control panels, unused for so long, and appraise the furnishings and fittings. Nothing had decayed: here on Elysium the ship had been preserved, free from corrosion and rot.

Yet that was not enough. As Matthew had long ago explained to Clifford and as he now explained to Alida, you could not leave a machine such as this ship unused for a couple of hundred years and expect it to work again as soon as you pressed a button. Circuits had to be checked, and innumerable mechanical adjustments made. Plates had buckled slightly, particularly around the exhausts, as a result of the mere weight of the ship remaining in the same position for so long. There were fuel problems, too: it was necessary to adapt the local supplies and to experiment with new combinations. The rocket tubes would need to be altered to cope with different conditions.

"Even so, it wouldn't be a difficult job," said Matthew, "if only we got some co-operation."

Alida did not reply. It was evident that she had not yet made up her mind whether to persist in regarding the whole venture as a pointless folly or whether to admit that, in spite of everything, her imagination was somehow fired.

As she climbed slowly and awkwardly up the slanting corridor to the main lounge, the two men looked out of an open port at the welders below. Clifford said:

"I was making a few more checks on that incoming planet just before you arrived."

"Oh, yes. Anything startling?"

"No It won't come very close. As far as my calculations go, I should say that it comes regularly into this area—about once in three hundred years, roughly. One of the travellers. That's assuming it has a fixed orbit, of course: it may be one of the rogues."

"In which case it might hit us."

"I don't think so. It won't even give us any bad weather, as far as I can tell."

"Any reports from any of the other towns?"

Clifford's lip curled. "Nobody else seems interested. Sometimes I can't even make radio contact with them—they don't answer calls, or else they leave their sets switched off altogether."

Matthew glanced at him with affection. He liked this boy. Clifford was one of the few speculative types left in this self-satisfied world. He was a scientist and an adventurer of the mind: he wanted to know why things happened; he wanted to make things work. He was driven on by a splendid discontent. In the old days, back on Earth, he would have been the sort of boy who at the age of three or four years takes a watch to pieces, and puts it back together again.

Suddenly Clifford leaned forward and muttered:

"Hello, what's the fuss?"

A man had run in from the direction of the observatory and was looking about him. Clifford shouted and waved.

The man below looked up and shouted.

"Can't hear a word," said Clifford. "Better go down. Bellhouse looks worked-up about something."

He slid expertly down the slope, caught the edge of the airlock door, and lowered himself down the flimsy ladder to the ground. He and Bellhouse talked for a moment, and then they were waving Matthew down. Matthew fetched Alida and helped her back to ground level. He found Clifford already fuming with impatience.

"A message from Martinstown," he said at once, as soon as Matthew had reached him. "Incredible. They've been attacked."

"Attacked? By whom?"

"Three spaceships."

Spaceships.... Matthew's first reaction was one of incredulous joy. Spaceships, messengers from home or at least from some civilisation in contact with Earth! Then the hope faded. It was too much to expect. And, as the meaning of what Clifford had said sank in, he demanded:

"But what reason was there for attacking Martinstown? Nobody on this planet would do it. Besides, we haven't got three spaceships anywhere

here. They're not things you can construct in secret. And who'd want to?"

"Nevertheless," said Clifford, "they reported a devastating attack on the town—a great blaze spreading from the outskirts, and the ships coming back for another attempt—and then they went dead. Not a sound. Cut off completely."

"I just don't understand. No race that I've ever known came out of the skies and starting destroying towns and people for no reason whatever. Was there no attempt to establish normal contact?"

"If there was," said Clifford grimly, "the operator didn't tell me. He said the ships circled low over the town for a minute or two; and of course everyone came out to have a look; and then the firing started."

They looked at one another, all possessed by the same thought at once.

Alida said: "We must tell our own people. At once."

Bellhouse went racing back to the observatory. The others followed, crossing the springy turf to the knoll on which the smaller building stood.

Clifford said, taking Alida's arm as they hurried up the steps: "Do you think they'll make for our own town now—or are the others to suffer first? We must send out a general alarm."

"If you can make anybody listen," said Matthew savagely. "If they haven't got their receivers switched off!"

They found Bellhouse already sending out his signal.

"No reply from our own administration Centre," he

snapped. "They've probably got their chairs drawn up to the window so they can admire the view—and the set switched off so that they're not disturbed by the demands of our modern mechanised civilisation."

He flicked another wavelength into operation, and got an immediate reply.

"Enemy spaceships attacked Martinstown," he said without delay.

There was a squawk of disbelief from the receiver.

"Martinstown has been blotted out," he shouted. "This is no joke. It's true. Best thing, maybe, is to get your people out into the woods and fields. Lie low until we see whether the ships are going to tackle any of the rest of us."

He cut off a protest in mid-sentence, and tried to make contact with the most remote of the Elysian towns. Again there was no reply. That could mean anything: it could mean that the set had been switched off, or it could mean that the town had already been destroyed.

"Perhaps it's going up in smoke this very minute," said Matthew. "But damn it, what's the point—?"

"They're coming! Here they come!"

The cry reached them faintly from below.

They swung round and looked up through the glass dome, over towards the hills that concealed the destruction of Martinstown.

There in the sky, speeding in this direction, were three slivers of brightness, three gleaming ships racing towards their own town.

"Outside!" snapped Clifford decisively. "Safer out there until we know what's happening. Down to the edge of the woods. You three get moving, I'll warn the others."

The men from the main construction hall were emerging into the open. Clifford waved them towards the shelter of the woods, then he himself stood for a moment at the foot of the slope, staring up as the ships came dropping lower and lower.

"Clifford!" It was Alida, despairingly calling him.

He waved reassuringly and moved slowly into cover, still watching with awed fascination as the ships streaked overhead, ignoring the two isolated buildings on the edge of the wood and heading straight for the town itself.

In less than ten seconds there was an explosion that shook the ground and sent a ravaging wind through the trees. Flame stood up in the distance, growing and bending, then growing again, like some lurching giant trying to stand upright.

Matthew said: "It's insane. So senseless.... Wanton destruction. What race can so lust for destruction that it attacks without provocation like this? Am I going mad?"

"If you are," said Clifford, "we all are."

Again there was a shudder through the earth. Beyond the trees, interlaced with the pattern of trunks and branches, they saw the great glow of their dying town.

Then they heard voices. A group of men and women, dragging and carrying children, forced their way through the undergrowth, sobbing and shouting with fear.

Alida moved towards them to offer help. Clifford waved to them to be careful and not to emerge from the wood yet.

Bellhouse began to sob with terrifying quietness. He said through his teeth: "My wife was in there. And my mother and father."

The flames began to attack the fringe of the woods.

Matthew said: "We won't be able to stay in here for long, once that fire gets started. It's to be hoped those ships have gone. If they're going to come back and destroy the observatory and the sheds, they'd better hurry up about it."

He stared down at the building that housed the space ship. If that went, all hope went with it. He was utterly impotent: he and this group of people with him could do nothing to check this murderous assault from the heavens.

Clifford said: "If they do come back...." He paused, and glanced questioningly at Matthew. "The disruptors—the guns on our ship—they work from the same power pile. It's still running on test. They ought to work."

Matthew said huskily: "Anything might go wrong. They haven't been checked over."

"Nothing much worse can happen than what's going to happen anyway," said Clifford. He took a pace forward, down the hill. "Are you coming?"

"Of course I'm coming."

Matthew, Clifford, and Bellhouse were running down to the entrance. They were breathless by the time they reached the control cabin, slipping and sliding along the tilted floor. Below, one of the men who had followed them threw a switch, and the great roof rolled back. Now the ship lay on its side beneath the sky to which it belonged. And inside the ship the three men watched and waited, each with fingers poised above the starboard disruptor controls.

"We shall probably go up along with the ship," said Bellhouse with a half-hysterical laugh.

Dazzling across the sky game the three destroyers, the three vicious ships from space. Their noses turned down towards the buildings that waited for there.

Clifford found time to say, as though it were a theory worth discussing at this very moment: "Maybe they come from that planet that's swum into view recently. Seems probable."

Matthew said: "Could be." And then the predictor control flickered its warning, the disruptor quivered gently and seemed to reach out as though plucked from its mountings by the approaching ships. Matthew's finger stabbed down.

There was a gout of savage, radiant force that scorched away part of the corner of the roof. But at the same time two stabbing fingers leaped out from the two companion disruptors, and caught in their mingled, blinding beam was one of the attacking ships.

It was knocked upwards as though punched by a mighty hand. The nose dissolved, molten metal falling on the ground below; and the spinning wreckage of what had once been a spaceship made a great spinning arc and came to earth out on the grassy plain below the hills.

"Next one!" shouted Matthews exultantly.

There was a delay. They waited for the other two ships to come back.

Then, faintly, they heard the mechanic calling them from below. Clifford opened the nearest port and leaned out.

"They've gone!" came the jubilant message.

"They'll only be turning to come back and have another go," warned Matthew.

"No. He says they've gone well beyond the hills— angled upwards."

"Off for reinforcements?"

"We can relax for a little while, anyhow."

Bellhouse stayed in the cabin in case of a sudden emergency. Matthew and Clifford lowered themselves to the ground and went out into the air, reeking with smoke that blew over from the stricken town. The woods were burning slowly but steadily.

The handful of survivors, helped down by the men who had been working here, came down to the shelter of the observatory.

Matthew said: "I think you're right, and those murderers did come from that new planet. Now they're going back to report. After all, from up there this ship of ours must look pretty menacing. It's four times as big as their things, and they couldn't know that it wasn't capable of leaving the ground. A couple of destroyers might be able to knock hell out of a battleship, but it's safer to go and get the rest of the fleet."

"I wonder how long that will take?"

"Hours, perhaps. Or maybe a day or two. I wouldn't be surprised to see them back tonight, ready to finish us off."

They looked out speculatively across the plain to the hills. It was Clifford who said:

"I'd like to go and have a look at that wreckage."

"What? Good heavens, yes."

"There might be somebody—something—still alive. We oughtn't to dismiss that possibility."

"After seeing that ship come down," said Matthew vindictively, "I am prepared to dismiss the possibility of anybody inside it being alive. But I'd like to have a look at what's left."

"Tomorrow," said Clifford, "we must investigate—if we're still alive. I think we need to be very much on the alert tonight."

* * * * * *

But the ships did not return that night. And in the morning it began to rain—not gently and refreshingly as it usually did on Elysium, but with a ferocity that literally beat the breath out of anybody not under cover. A wind came up—a wind such as had never been known on this planet before. Then lightning blazed along the horizon, heralding a furious electrical storm that lasted for five days.

It was futile to try to contact the other towns, to find if they still existed. There was nothing but a wild roaring in the receiver. Light played about the observatory dome, and the hall in which the spaceship lay resounded to the persistent drumming of the rain.

"There used to be a lot of arguments back on Earth," Matthew reminisced, "about the effects of man's doings. There were tales told of the really ancient days when cannons were fired at clouds to bring rain down. And then bad weather was blamed on atom bombs and so on. It may or may not have been true on Earth, but it certainly looks as though the weapons we—or maybe those others—used here have shaken up the Elysian atmosphere."

Clifford said: "It's saved us from an immediate attack, anyway. I don't believe any ship would try any nonsense under these conditions."

"We'll just have to wait and see what happens when the storm clears."

At the end of the fifth day there were signs that stability was returning. The rain stopped and the electric oppressiveness of the atmosphere relaxed its grip on the men and women who had been sheltering in the construction hall. The skies cleared. Clifford did not waste any time. He went to the observatory, and returned within fifteen minutes, pursing his lips over a sheet of scribbled calculations.

"That planet has moved some distance away by now," he said. "My guess is that we won't see any more of those ships. There was a sharp intersection of our two orbits, but we're moving away from one another pretty fast, and I should imagine that the distance is too great for them to make another sortie like that— unless, of course, they're really anxious to make a lot of trouble."

"I still can't begin to understand that first attack," said Matthew. "I don't see how we shall ever find out what it was all about."

Clifford said: "We can start with that wrecked ship. If they don't come back and attack us again tonight, now that it's clear again, we must go over to the hills tomorrow morning and examine the wreckage."

"Before we do that," said Matthew sombrely, "we shall have to go and have a look at the town. There can't be any more survivors: we should have had them over here in no time at all. But we must go and see exactly what happened to the town."

It was a grim duty that faced them on that following morning. They stepped in silent horror over the crumpled ruins of what had so recently been graceful buildings. Charred bodies lay on the edge of once-beautiful gardens. On the slopes below the Community Palace, the fountains still played. But the young men and women would not walk here again.

The rain had extinguished all the fires, and at the same time had carried black rivulets across lawns and across the whiteness of fallen masonry. The town had become smeared and ugly in its death throes.

Matthew said abruptly: "There's nothing we can do here. Nothing but go away and leave it."

Clifford said: "Oughtn't we to...? I mean...."

He fumbled, unsure of himself, and Matthew said: "You want a handful of us to try to give decent burial to all the bits and pieces we can find? To sweep up the bits? It couldn't be done. Don't think I'm callous, Clifford. I'm just trying to be realistic."

The young man nodded.

"While we're being realistic," he said, "I think we ought to face up to the fact that the few helicars we had in this town have all been destroyed. Unless we can catch an Elysian pony—which is unlikely—we shall have to walk in order to reach that wreckage. And I suggest we start now."

Three of them went—Matthew, Clifford, and Bellhouse. After reporting to the others and warning them to be careful if they proposed to explore the ruins for personal belongings, they set off on the long walk across the plain.

It was a warm day, and by the time they had finished the five or six miles, they were hot and weary. They stopped a hundred yards away from the fallen spaceship, and looked at it speculatively.

Matthew said: "Better be careful."

There was no sound from the interior. No sound, no movement.

Clifford abruptly strode forward, indicating that the other two should stay where they were. He went up to the jagged opening where the nose had been blown off.

They saw him peer in. Then he stepped cautiously over the raw edges of torn metal, and disappeared from their sight inside the remains of the hull.

CHAPTER THREE

Light fell obliquely through holes and shattered ports. Clifford picked his way over a tangle of wiring and metal fragments. In the comer he saw a torn heap of something that was not metallic—something that might once have been a living being.

The horrors of the morning's investigation had hardened him. He looked down with no more than a slight, involuntary contraction of his throat at the pulped flesh. Whatever it had once been, it was nothing human: it was an alien, unrecognisable creature.

He turned away and was about to open the door that hung loosely across the corridor when he heard a faint scratching noise.

Clifford stood quite still.

It came again, faint but unmistakable.

He moved cautiously along the wall and reached silently towards the door. Then he kicked it open and went through.

Below a control panel that formed the whole of one wall lay something that was alive—just alive.

It scrabbled long, fine claws against the floor, and made a guttural noise that might have been a word or a groan of pain.

It was a creature that did not seem to belong to the order of vertebrates as men knew it. There was a slackness about its whole bulky body that reminded Clifford of some reptile—only the body was grey and possessed none of the beautiful flickering colours of the Elysian reptiles. The head was flattened and marked out with a pattern of scaly flaps that might have been eyes or other sensory organs. Incongruously, the mouth might have been a human mouth, though it was thicker and more fleshy than any human mouth had ever been.

Clifford bent over the creature. The weak throbbing and twisting of its body testified to its agony. Even with the memory of the destroyed town fresh in his mind, he instinctively sought for some way to alleviate this being's pain.

But before he could even begin to think of what could be done, the creature spoke. It spoke to him in his own language. It said in a thick slurring voice:

"Earthman.... Go away. Do not touch me. I wish to die unpolluted."

Clifford stood up, dumbfounded. His first impulse was to fire questions, to demand why such a murderous attack had been made on the towns of Elysium. Before he could speak, the creature thrust itself up into an ungainly mound, struggling to rise to its strangely flexing legs.

"I die hating you," it mouthed. "We did well before you struck us. We destroyed nobly, and it is good. Conquerors, exploiters...your day has come."

"Now, hold it a minute," said Clifford. "I want to know what—"

The voice rose to a scream. "Hatred of your people is a sacred duty, and we of this ship have done our duty. The day of reckoning is here. You shall be wiped from the universe."

The effort had been too much. It slumped down and did not move again.

There were other voices—familiar, reassuring voices—calling Clifford's name. The two men outside were getting worried. He went further along the corridor and found the airlock door, pulled away from its mountings. He opened it, and Matthew and Bellhouse climbed in.

Clifford led them into what was obviously the control cabin, and showed them the dead mass on the floor. He repeated what he had heard.

"There must be some others aboard. Perhaps one or two were quite blotted out when the nose was hit, but there must be some in the stern of the ship."

Warily, they explored the rest of the small craft. They found six more bodies. Bellhouse shuddered.

"Hideous things. They're not natural."

Matthew chuckled. "There are stranger things than that in the universe. Actually, this is a life-form that I've seen once or twice—or variations of it, that is." He frowned thoughtfully. "These creatures remind me of something. I believe there were such beings on one of the outer worlds. They were friendly when we arrived. We left a fairly large group of our people there to establish good relations, so that trade possibilities could be opened up when a good regular service had been established with Earth. They were friendly," he repeated.

"They certainly aren't friendly any longer," said

Clifford. "Come on, let's see what we can find out about the ship itself. The controls and the drive chambers don't seem to have suffered too badly. We might find out something useful."

Bellhouse said: "It's very doubtful if we can follow the workings of an alien mind. Their engines and indicators won't mean a thing to us."

"Perhaps not, but there's no harm in trying to sort out a few loose ends."

He examined the dials on the control panel, and then looked down at a chart on the slanting panel at which two pilots obviously sat.

"If only we knew what this meant."

"I once had a head for figures," said Matthew self-consciously. "Surely we can find some relation between their figures and our own. Mathematics can't vary."

"I'm not sure that I believe in mathematical absolutes," said Clifford, "but I'm willing to make the effort."

They were in a way, thought Matthew, complementary: Clifford had an urge to know, to pull things to pieces, to drag the truth forcibly out of things; he himself had lived too long to be impatient—he saw things in perspective, set them in their places, and worked methodically.

They worked in the ship until the late afternoon, Bellhouse spending most of his time in the cramped engine-room, the other two comparing charts and trying to make sense of the characters on the displays. When they decided to call it a day, they had reached certain conclusions—conclusions that made them shake their heads incredulously. Bellhouse, coming in from the engine-room, said:

"It's queer. I can't make out what all that stuff in there is supposed to do, and yet I can guess what a lot of the components are for."

Matthew and Clifford exchanged glances.

"You mean that the—er—well, what you might call basic elements are the same as our own?" asked Clifford.

"Something like that. They must have a different way of making the ship move from what we have, but the machinery isn't at all strange."

Clifford nodded. "It's more or less the same is here," he said. "The symbols aren't the same as ours, but it's only a matter of mathematical transposition. These displays are easy to read, though of course we don't know the actual value of the quantities represented: we only know—and recognise—the proportions, the relation of one symbol to another. There's even a clock here: and I'm willing to swear it's based on the same principles as our own clocks."

Matthew hastened to agree. "After seeing the linear clocks of Antares and some of the weird devices used by other races," he said, "it hits you in the eye when you come across a clock that looks like a clock."

"What it amounts to," murmured Clifford, "is that these creatures started from the same basic suppositions as the builders of our own space ship—of our own civilisation, even. It's not just that they worked away at a problem and came to the same conclusion; they started out the same. There's a family likeness in everything here that can't be mistaken. Everything fits into our own scheme of knowledge. And that dying creature spoke to me in our own language. It's as though he were a member of a race that had been educated by Earthmen, taught to cope with things as Earthmen cope with them. This race may have learned its groundwork from Earthmen, just as a musical genius-to-be learns his basic theory from a teacher; and then they've developed these techniques further—"

"And then," Matthew continued, "they've turned against their benefactors."

"If they were benefactors," said Clifford.

"What are you getting at?"

"I don't know. It was a thought that came into my head. I'm not really sure," he frankly laughed, "that I know what I mean. I was just groping."

They looked at the array of displays on the control panel as though expecting them to surrender their meaning at once.

Clifford went on: "But what's so impossible is that if these figures we've worked out mean anything at all—and they tally in every way—this ship travels at a speed that...that...well," he waved his right hand vaguely, "we've never believed in such a thing."

Matthew said: "It's no good pretending we're not sure. We're quite certain. These figures can't lie. We've worked out the relationship between the clock symbols, those four displays above the scanner, and this heap of charts, and we know we've worked it out right. And if these figures mean what we think they mean—what we're damned sure they mean—then a ship powered by these engines could reach Earth in twenty-five years."

Bellhouse shook his head dazedly. He said: "But that means—"

"It means," said Matthew, "that if we could transfer the engines to our own ship, or adapt them for our own use, everyone on board could reach Earth alive. Not just myself, and not the descendants of the original crew, but all those who actually embark!"

They went out into the open air and looked up at the stars that were already bright in the first haze of twilight.

Clifford said: "We don't know how those engines work. We don't know how seriously damaged they are. We don't know if they will work in a larger ship such as ours. But by heaven, we're going to find out. I want to see Earth and find out what has been happening. The prospect of seeing Earth itself was only a dream, but now it's a possibility. And by the time we've finished it will be a probability!"

* * * * * *

They worked for three months on exasperating preparations that had to be made before the real work could be tackled. Men whose work would have been welcomed full-time on the mechanical side had to spend a certain amount of time on the land, maintaining food supplies for present requirements and preparing concentrates for the journey. Most of the food would of course be grown on board by the shallow culture method, providing concentrates in sufficient quantity to feed the crew effectively. Someone had to make experiments with this technique, as none of those at present available were experts on such matters.

Fortunately, at the end of the first month, an experienced biologist appeared. He came trudging into sight across the plain in company with four others—survivors of Decelonia, the town beyond Martinstown.

"We heard your signals and questions on the day of the attack," he told Matthew and Clifford, "but after that the building was destroyed, and we had no way of getting in touch with you."

He and his companions had come through Martinstown and found no one left alive there. But from the hills they had seen the shattered enemy ship, and signs of activity in the distance, and they had come on full of hope.

"Must have been different ships that attacked you," said Clifford after a comparison of times on that fateful day had been made. "Mm. They were certainly out to finish us off."

The biologist gladly set to work to develop the shallow culture beds. Three of the women who had come with him began to make clothing. "We shall wear as little as possible on board ship," Matthew explained. "You'll find it gets intolerably hot inside the ship, even though space itself is icy cold. But the climates of other planets are nothing like Elysium. We must have plenty of adequate clothing stowed away, ready for when we need it." And so the various tasks were allotted to eager helpers. Setting off into space was not merely a matter of building a suitable engine into a ship, and then launching it: food and clothing, air purification plant and the manufacture of oxygen in conjunction with the food culture shelves were all prime essentials.

Innumerable frustrating difficulties were encountered. A prosperous industrial civilisation had first conceived and built the spaceship that had left Earth for the stars. A pastoral civilisation whose members had nearly all been blotted out in a ruthless attack was now trying to make that ship spaceworthy again, and it was not an easy task. The months rolled by. The furnaces in the old factories on the far side of the town had to be brought into use, and their inefficiencies rectified.

Clifford and Bellhouse spent weeks tracing the convolutions of the drive mechanism in the enemy ship. They evolved a theory, experimented, and nearly blew out the side of the main building. But they insisted that they were on the right track, and went on until they were satisfied.

Matthew found it hard now to control his impatience. Despite all the setbacks, his dream of going home was nearer realisation than it had ever been before; but that only had the effect of making him more and more irritable. How long would these wearisome constructional jobs take? How long before they soared up into space and turned towards Earth?

There were other problems to be dealt with, too. Human problems.

Most of those preparing for the flight into space had been enthusiasts from the start. The nucleus of the group was formed of men and women whose imaginations had been excited by Matthew's hopes and by the stories he told, and now that their homes had been destroyed they had an additional reason for no longer staying on this planet. Added to that, the promise of getting to Earth in twenty-five years was a real incentive.

But there were one or two people who were not too happy about the voyage. Two young men and a middle-aged woman who had come from Decelonia were particularly hostile.

"Why should we slave to go out and spend the better part of our lives cooped up in a spaceship?" they demanded. "Better to stay here. We can live simply, and slowly rebuild a town here."

"A hundred years from now," grumbled the woman, "there could be a thriving town here again—or at the very least a village—instead of nothing at all. If we set off in this ship, we may all be killed, and there will be nothing left on Elysium but ruins. But if we stay, in a few hundred years there will be happiness and life here again—"

"And in a few hundred years," said Clifford, "that planet will come swimming back along its orbit, and the destroying ships may come again. They may come along before then, because new drives will have been perfected—and new weapons of destruction."

"Well, it won't be in my lifetime, anyway," said the woman.

It was not easy to be patient with such people. Nor did it do any good to smile calmly and say that they could stay behind if they wished: they became rapidly abusive, as though it had been suggested that they should be brutally murdered or left to starve.

And in addition to this small group, there were one or two waverers. There was, for example, Alida.

Matthew saw Alida frequently, as he went to and fro in the clamour of each energetic day, and each time he saw her his envy of Clifford increased. The girl had such a brittle, fragile appearance, and yet was so taut and full of vitality. It was not often that she smiled, but that slow reflective parting of her lips was worth waiting for. Even Elysium had rarely produced a creature so beautiful.

And she did not want to leave Elysium.

In the evening, when the clangour and confusion around the spaceship had ceased, Matthew would sometimes see her walking in the shadows of the wood with Clifford, They walked slowly, and talked spasmodically, in an intimate undertone. Sometimes Clifford would be moody the next day.

On one such occasion Matthew decided to tackle the matter openly. He strolled up the slope as Clifford and Alida emerged from the woods, and waited for them to join him.

The evening light cast a glow on Alida's bare arms.

She looked up at the splashes of colour that lay across the sky, and then glanced out across the plain as though anxious to fix it all in her memory—as though reluctant ever to be forced to leave it.

Matthew said: "You two look glum. Getting tired of waiting for the ship to be finished?"

Alida sensed the irony in his tone if Clifford didn't and she said at once: "It breaks my heart to think of leaving here. These wonderful evenings; the afternoons of summer; the sounds and scents of this world...."

"I should have thought," said Matthew quietly, "that the sight of the town ruins would have depressed you. There would always be too many memories here."

"We could go away. There are thousands of miles of the planet that have never been travelled at all."

"But wherever you go on this planet, one day the ships will come back, and there will be destruction once more—if not for you, for those who come after you."

Sadly she nodded. "I know that well. I know that we must go. But it's so hard. To turn your back on beauty and resign yourself to imprisonment for twenty-five years is a bitter thing."

Matthew tried to point out that they would not be in space for the whole time. They would stop on the way: they would visit other worlds and try to make contact with the other races, to find out what had happened to the pioneers from Earth who had been left behind on that outward journey. None had ever come on to Elysium: that was not surprising, as the leap to Elysium had been the longest and most arduous stretch of all; but one wanted to know, to learn, to be told the innumerable histories.

Alida nodded her acceptance of all that he said. She would come with Clifford—there was no question of that—but she did not pretend that she was happy. Her imagination had once been kindled by the enthusiasm of the two men, but that spurt of interest had been overcome by her longing for the tranquility of life on the world she knew so well.

Leaving them, Matthew found himself wondering if he was justified in driving these people so hard. If he were to cease harrying them, they would not leave Elysium. With the pressure relaxed, they would fall into their old ways. Even Clifford, drawn into contentment with Alida, would probably not persist for long. The ship would remain where it was, almost ready for a take-off that it would never make.

Was he, Matthew, wrong: was he being as selfish as many people had accused him of being in the past, and as one or two still accused him of being?

"Home," he said softly to himself. They could not understand what the conception meant.

Yet, was that true? To them, this was home. He was urging them to leave their home merely in order to accompany him on a voyage back to an old world they had never known and could hardly be expected to love.

He walked past the observatory and stood brooding over the darkening plain.

Somewhere a girl laughed, and a young man longingly called her name.

Why not let them stay? The murderous ships might come back, but that was no immediate concern of these people here today. Things might have changed. Whatever had prompted these strange beings to launch such a vicious assault might not have any effect a couple of hundred years from now. It might be safer to stay here and take a chance—or let one's descendants take a chance—than to go out into space in a reconditioned spaceship whose behaviour was, to say the least of it, unpredictable.

And then what of his dreams: what would remain for Matthew then?

The same life as before. He would help in the rebuilding of the community, knowing that on a planet like this, where living was easy, there would never be ambition, never any knowledge of the hopes and fears that he had known. At first, surrounded by this small group who regarded him with some respect, he would be a person of some consequence. But as the decades rolled past, there would be the inevitable decline. His histories would be laughed at as fables. Even his story of the attack from space, and his warnings of a possible recurrence, would become blurred and distorted. They would say he was telling fairy stories and that there had never been any such attack. They would find reasons for not listening to him. Realisation that he was considered a bore would creep over him again.

Death, then?

He felt a cold chill strike at his heart. The older he

grew and the more tired he became of existence, the more he shrank from death. He was not a coward, but his instincts were not under the control of his mind. For a young man to commit suicide is difficult: a human being has to fight every natural impulse in order to put an end to his own life; but for a man of Matthew's age, the instinctive rejection of such a course was a hundred, a thousand times stronger than normal. That way out was a defeat—a defeat he could not, would not accept.

He knew that, selfish or not, he was going to go on: he was going to strike out on the long way back home. Nothing else was possible. They would go, all of them... and, he vowed, they would get there.

CHAPTER FOUR

At last they were ready. The ship lay out in the open, the launching cradle pointing it to the stars. Final preparations were made. Everything had been checked and double-checked, but still Matthew was pale with apprehension. Nothing could go wrong now: nothing must go wrong.

All possible stores had been taken aboard. It was now their last night on Elysium.

And during that last afternoon, a ceremony had taken place. Alida and Clifford had gone through the simple, formal ritual of the Elysian marriage agreement.

"The last wedding on Elysium," commented one of the women sentimentally.

They all felt sentimental at that time. The risks they were about to take assumed colossal proportions. Matthew would not have been surprised if there had been an attempt to call the expedition off, even at this late date; but it seemed as though, now they had got this far, they were all determined to go through with it.

He and Clifford made a final check of their calculations. Tomorrow the lives of all of them would depend on the accuracy and relevance of those figures. If the two men had been working on false assumptions, or if Bellhouse and the mechanics had failed to comprehend fully the machinery that had been so laboriously adapted and built into this ship, they might in a matter of seconds be no more than a sudden spark in the sky, a molten mass falling back to the surface of Elysium or dropping forever through the vastness of space.

The ship vibrated, humming a tune to itself as Bellhouse made his last adjustments. Power throbbed in the heart of it, still leashed but ready to shake off restraint and hurl the ship outward.

The principle of the drive, they had discovered, was not a mere crude thrusting forward such as had been employed in the original Earth-made vessel. It relied on a twisting of the natural tensions of the cosmos. The stresses that held the universe together were all utilised, as a man might use any handhold he could find to make his way along a dangerous precipice. The creatures who had designed this space drive had adapted gravitational pulls and the force fields of different galaxies to their own uses. The ship would pursue a strange, erratic course that would neverthe-less bring it to its destination sooner than if it had followed a straight line. Ricocheting, leaping from one system to another like a man throwing himself reck-lessly from one springboard to another, it would twist itself at incredible speed through the mesh of inter-woven forces and gravitational fields that preserved the balance of the universe.

"Well," said Clifford at last, his eyes tired, "we can't do any more. We ought to get some sleep."

"You'd better go and comfort your wife," said Matthew. "She hates to leave Elysium."

"So do I, in a way. But in another way...."

He left the sentence unfinished, but he and Matthew exchanged an affectionate smile. They were both weary, yet both excited. They shared the exultation of knowing that at last the attempt was to be made.

Matthew remained in the control room for some minutes after Clifford had gone. Then he sighed, clam-bered down the great length of the hull to the ground, and looked up at the massive shape against the sky.

"Tomorrow," he said softly. "Tomorrow."

Then he went to bed, and slept a fitful, disturbed sleep gashed by many dreams.

In the morning there was too much bustle for there to be any time for regrets. Each of the thirty members of the crew turned at the airlock to take a last quick glance at the sunlit world; and then they were inside, strapping themselves to the sprung seats which would later be distributed throughout the ship, but which were for the present bolted to the floor of the communal lounge, facing towards the nose of the ship.

Matthew and Clifford sat side by side at the control panel. They thumbed the various relays to make sure that all the ports were closed, the whole vessel sealed up.

"Shall we go?" said Clifford with a strained, unreal laugh.

"Take her up," said Matthew.

The engine room light glowed its readiness. A gentle shudder began to murmur through the length of the ship. A note starting at a low frequency rose like a faint far-off siren, and then was lost.

Clifford watched the dial before him, and then said: "This is it."

The pressure of his thumb released a force that seemed to strike them in the stomach. Breath went, sight and hearing were blotted out, and for thirty seconds there was nothing in existence but pain and constriction, a desperate struggle to fill the lungs and not to give way to panic as blood pounded in the head.

The intolerable pressure mounted. Then it was as though the ship had looped the loop. Everything went round. Matthew felt that his insides were being tossed about and jumbled up so that he would never be able to sort them out again. He knew that he was trying to say something to Clifford, but had not the faintest idea what it could be.

And then the pain died away. Bones were left aching, and Matthew felt that his head would split open, but the awful weight against his chest and stomach had gone.

He said: "Free."

Clifford leaned his forehead against the cool panel in front of him.

"We're caught in the galactic flux," he said. "So far so good. Theory and practice have tied up—so far."

They looked at one another, and both of them had, absurdly, tears in their eyes.

From then on the main problem was an administrative one. The ship, moving at a fantastic speed through space, did not seem to its occupants to be moving at all. There were no landmarks and no sensation of movement. It was as though this scrap of metal and its human cargo were hanging motionless in infinity, lost in the star-studded vastness. There was no sense of danger: the only danger was boredom, and Matthew knew how serious that would become as time went on.

Looking at the stars through the glassite ports was a pastime that soon palled. The stars were fixed and immutable. They were apparently always in the same position: the ship did not approach them; no planets swam past, and there was no difference between night and day.

"We shall be all right for a little while," said Matthew to Clifford, "and we must do all we can to foster friendships and—er—romances on board ship. The biologist, Richard, already enjoys the company of that woman who made such a fuss about leaving. If they marry, that'll keep them occupied for a few years before they get really fretful."

"You make it sound very matter-of-fact," said Clifford ruefully.

"We can't afford to be anything but realistic. The first world that we're headed for will take five years to reach. We've got to keep our tempers somehow for five years."

There were thirty people aboard—ten women, twenty men, and two children. The six men who had been trained as pilots took their turns, two at a time, in the control cabin. This was mainly a matter of routine: held to its predicted course, the ship ran itself smoothly, but a constant watch was necessary in case a meteorite shower or some other unexpected phenomenon threatened.

The engine-room maintenance staff worked in similar shifts. Dr. Richard was fully occupied with the food culture shelves and the issue of concentrate capsules.

The women were the real trouble—or they would be, in time. Although each one was allotted a task, they still had time on their hands. Sitting in the communal lounge, they talked until it seemed there was nothing left to talk about, and then bickered irritably. Matthew had made sure that several sets of Elysian Tarasco cards had been manufactured before they left, and involved games of this were played for months on end. But the games became acrimonious, and there were perpetual outbreaks of hostility between different cliques—cliques to which the men as well as the women belonged.

As Matthew had predicted, the unmarried women were soon paired off with men of the crew. One of the two children who had come along was an attractive little girl who would undoubtedly prove a source of rivalry in a few years' time.

And after the marriages had taken place, it was inevitable that surreptitious affairs should commence—flirtations and passionate attachments that could not be kept secret for long in the cramped space of the ship.

"As long as nobody gets thrown out of the airlock, I suppose we mustn't complain," remarked Clifford. But Matthew observed that the young man guarded his wife Alida jealously. He gossiped freely about the behaviour of other members of the crew, when he and Matthew were on duty together, but he would have been the first to start violence if anyone had made advances to Alida.

New games of cards were invented as they went on. One of the men had a fine voice and an imaginative gift for versifying, and he sang songs that had much in common with old primitive ballads: he set the memories of all of them to music, filling them with nostalgia as he dwelt on the beauties of the planet they had left. Matthew did not actively discourage this, but he hinted at one time that it would be better for everyone's morale if the singer could turn out some bright prophetic verses about the worlds they would visit in the future rather than about the one to which they could not return.

Week succeeded week, month trickled down upon meaningless month. They were one year out from

Elysium; then two years.

One of the engineers had a fit of hysteria and would have smashed his hands to pulp against the unyielding side of the ship if Dr. Richards had not forced a sedative preparation down his throat.

Two men fought over the wife of one of them, and provided food for conversation for nearly a fortnight.

Gradually the star patterns in the sky shifted slightly.

A child was born to the wife of Dr. Richard. It was a boy. The women of the company showered attentions on him: no child had ever been so spoilt. But Matthew was glad to see him, and hoped, that there would be more. A new life always uplifted the dullest and weariest people. It brought with it hope and a sort of promise that they all recognised without being able to explain.

But there was still too much time to fill each day. Sleep, to which so many resorted, did not come easily. They none of them did enough work to be really tired, and they did not possess the hibernating faculty of certain animals. One day, thought Matthew, it will be possible, perhaps, to put ourselves to sleep for several years, and cross space in what seems a matter of seconds.

Trouble of some sort was bound to break out. It came from two of the men—the two who had opposed the idea of leaving Elysium in the first place.

They came into the control cabin when Matthew and Clifford were on duty. It was during the sleep period: it was still called 'night' although the eternity outside made no difference between day and night.

Matthew glanced up and tensed at once, sensing trouble.

He said: "Only pilots should be in here."

"That's a ruling that you yourself laid down. We're getting a bit tired of doing things your way."

It was the taller of the two who spoke, a lean and resentful-looking man with a nervous habit of chewing his thin lips.

Clifford said: "We are all agreed that Matthew is the man who should make decisions."

"Not all of us. We're tired. We're tired of this whole mad business."

"We're all tired," said Clifford in a level voice. "It's just a matter of carrying on."

"Is it? That's what we want to settle. We don't think it's any such thing."

The other man said aggressively: "There's such a thing as turning back."

"You must be mad," said Matthew.

"It's going on that's the madness. We've been talking to some of the women, and it's wearing them down. They can't take it. They want to get back to their homes. We've wasted over two years. We want to cut our losses and turn back to Elysium."

"Back to Elysium?" Matthew echoed furiously. "You don't know what you're talking about. We're committed to this trip now, and we're going on. In any case—"

"I say we're going back!"

The man's voice had risen to a scream. The two of them suddenly sprang on Clifford and Matthew. Clifford was taken by surprise, and went over sideways. But Matthew had been braced for some such thing from the moment the two men came into the room. He struck out decisively, and sent the shouting, cursing man back across the room.

The one who had dislodged Clifford from his chair made a wild, insane grab at the control panel. Matthew grabbed his arm and pulled him away. Clifford, rolling over on his side, reached for the man's ankles, and brought him down with a heavy thud on the hard floor.

"That'll be all!" said Matthew harshly.

Breathing painfully, the two men stood sheepishly against the wall. The madness had been knocked out of them, but they were not prepared to give up their argument.

The taller of the two, his lip twitching, said:

"You can't go on holding us all forever, you know. Sooner or later everyone on board will be in here, insisting that you turn round and go back."

Matthew gave a snort of exasperation. "It's not a question of going back. We're not just coasting down a straight road. We can't turn round and start travelling in the opposite direction. We're geared to a sequence of force fields—we pushed off from Elysium and we've got to keep jumping, following the sequence that was calculated in advance. When you jump from a trapeze you don't try to turn round in mid-air and get back."

Mention of a trapeze meant nothing to them, but

they grudgingly accepted the truth of what he had said.

"But when we get to this planet that we're visiting on the way? Couldn't we start back from there?"

"Yes," said Matthew bluntly. "We could set up new co-ordinates and push ourselves off in the direction of Elysium. But for what purpose? It will take five years to get from Elysium to the first world we're going to visit, and then if yon turned back it would take another five years. Ten years wasted. Why not go on now that you've started?"

"Why shouldn't we settle down on this world we're going to reach? If it's habitable, and if there's already a colony there, or if the natives are friendly, why shouldn't we stay there?"

Clifford said: "You can do that, if you want to. When we reach this planet, we'll discuss it. Those who want to stay can stay."

For the time being the rebellious malcontents had to be satisfied with that. When they had left the cabin, Matthew said to Clifford:

"That was a rash promise. We'd made no arrangement about people stopping off on the way."

"It's the best thing to tell them. We can cut the crew to half and still operate the ship, if necessary. And it's better to leave the faint-hearted behind than to risk a mutiny. You'll find that there won't be many who'll stay—and those who do stay will be replaced in due course by the children who grow up during the voyage. Dr. Richard's boy will be a young man by the time we reach Earth."

Matthew nodded his agreement.

He noticed during the days that followed that Clifford made several references to this question of children being born and growing to maturity aboard the space ship. In a little while he guessed the reason.

Halfway between Elysium and the first planet they were to visit, Alida presented her husband with a daughter.

Once more the women of the ship were delighted. And the arrival of this daughter had a very good effect on Alida herself. The sadness that she had never been able to shake off when they said goodbye to Elysium was now less noticeable. She was fully occupied with Eve, as the girl was called. The pallor of her fine high cheeks, inevitable in the living conditions of the space ship, seemed less marked: there was at least a flush of happiness to give a touch of colour to her face.

Matthew was glad for her sake and Clifford's, but at the same time he had to admit that he himself felt lonelier than he had done before. He and Clifford shared duties as before, but now he felt somehow remoter from his young friend. Clifford and Alida and their child belonged to another world. Whatever troubles they might have, they would never know anything like Matthew's loneliness.

The years stretched ahead, as hazy in the distance as the great nebulae that sprawled across the heavens. Down through space and time twisted the ship.

Until at last it approached the system in which lay the planet, the first port of call, for whose solid ground and clear atmosphere they had been longing. Dazzlingly framed in the observation port was a bright sun, and round it moved four planets. The ship fell into an orbit round the outer one of these four worlds. Gradually it sank through the fine trailing clouds. Continents opened up beneath it.

But they were dead continents—vast tracts of slaughter and devastation.

* * * * * * *

They landed on the outskirts of a shattered city. Nothing moved in the ruins. The bright sun shone mercilessly on the bleached heaps of masonry and the splintered columns of what had once been magnificent buildings.

Before opening the airlock, Matthew tested for radioactivity or the presence of any other lingering force that might prove harmful; but the instrument panel stayed reassuringly negative.

Clifford said: "This is a wonderful welcome, I must say. After all the talk there's been these past few months—as though we were going on a carefree holiday—and now look at this!"

The biologist and Matthew were the first to leave the ship. They stood for a minute or two surveying the expanse of silent ruins; then Matthew said:

"I don't think there's any chance of an enemy lurking anywhere in that lot. All this happened a good time ago—some years ago, I'd say."

The others came out cautiously into the open air.

Despite the depressing sight of the crumpled city, so reminiscent of the debris they had left on their own world five years ago, they could not help exulting in the sense of freedom after all this time. One of the women fainted, and Matthew had to admit that he himself felt dizzy.

"We'd better not poke about in the ruins," said Clifford. "We don't want to fall into hidden cellars or pull anything down on top of ourselves. But I think we ought to take the ship up and visit one or two other of the cities we saw as we came down. There may be somebody left."

Matthew shook his head thoughtfully. "They all looked much the same from the air. And we can't afford to waste fuel like that. You know what a colossal drain it is, using power to force the ship through a planet's atmosphere on mere reconnaissance work."

Clifford nodded. "We could try sending out a radio signal, and making a regular waveband check to see if there are any incoming signals."

Alida came up to him, her daughter staggering along over the uneven ground, holding on to her left hand.

"Before making plans of any sort," said Alida gently, "can't we spend a few days enjoying the fresh air?"

"She's talking sense," agreed Matthew. "Let's make the most of things for a day or two. We can do any exploring later. Let's enjoy being alive and on solid ground. And later," he added drily, "we can see if anybody wants to stay here permanently."

One group of men and women wanted to spend the

night sleeping out in the open. It had been a common practice during the months of the Elysian summer, and the sun here was so warm that it would surely be safe to do so here.

Matthew disapproved. The day here was warm, but the nights might be cold. After having adjusted themselves to the stable temperature of the ship, it would be stupid to run unnecessary risks. For the first night they would sleep on board, and guards would be posted. The guards could report on the temperature.

His doubts were justified. The night was cold, and a strong wind blew from the distant mountains.

The next morning groups of two or three went off for walks. "Not too far," Matthew warned them. He knew that he was regarded as a dismal killjoy, always raising objections; but he knew also that none of them was in good enough condition for more than mild doses of physical exertion, and that they could all tire themselves out too easily.

Despite instructions, the children escaped into the ruins, and one of them twisted an ankle.

At the end of the third day, Clifford again urged that they should expend a certain amount of fuel in a trip over the continents of this world. They must find out if there was nothing left alive. And somewhere there ought to be some indication of why this dreadful destruction had taken place.

They travelled above the remains of cities, flying low, and found no sign of any living being. But in one expanse of ruins they found dead bodies, thrown clear of falling buildings. Some of them were human beings; others were the bodies of four-legged creatures with large heads and furry backs. It looked as though the humans and these others had lived together on equal terms. Certainly they had died together.

And at last, on the outskirts of a small town near which the ship had landed because it stood near a refreshing inland sea, there was a sign of movement.

It was Bellhouse who saw the creature. He was standing with Dr. Richard on the shore while the biologist took samples of the water for testing. They had turned to look back at the ship, lying on the far side of the white town, and suddenly Bellhouse said:

"Something moved. There. Over there."

They stood quite still and waited.

There was a cautious movement in the shadows of what might once have been a temple or a theatre. It was repeated. Very slowly a small animal—or was it something more than an animal, some higher form of life?—came out into the open. It was about three feet high, walking forward on short legs and seeming to lean over slightly as though ready to touch the ground and balance itself with its long, swaying arms. The sun shone brightly into its face. It turned its head from side to side as though dazzled.

Then it stopped. It shaded its eyes with a curving arm, and looked straight at the two men.

The noise it made was indescribable. It was a scream: and whatever differences there might be between life on this planet and life on the world that Bellhouse and the doctor had known, both of them would have been prepared to swear that the scream was one of undiluted terror.

"Its hair stood on end," said Bellhouse afterwards. "It associated us with something it knew...and hated."

In a flash it had gone, burrowing back into the ruins. They heard it cry out once more, perhaps issuing a warning to others that crouched in the shadows or cellars. Bellhouse hurried back to report.

"What has happened?" asked Clifford for the hundredth time. "Is there some race that has travelled through the universe intent on destruction? Elysium was attacked and our people massacred. Here a whole civilisation has been destroyed. If anyone is left alive, there's no sign apart from this one we've just had: if there are any human beings, they are in hiding."

Matthew said slowly: "Remembering what that creature in the spaceship said just before it died, I'm beginning to think there has been a deadly war. A rebellion of some sort, followed by war. And the human race isn't too popular. That thing Bellhouse and Richard saw, whatever it was, was terrified. What had human beings done to it in the past—or what sort of upheaval did it associate with human beings?"

"If it's like this all the way across the universe...."

In all their minds was the mutual agreement that they must leave this planet. Even the men who had once talked of staying and settling down felt that the bleakness of destruction was too demoralising: the only thing to do was to go on.

One fearful question nagged at them: what would they find at their next stopping place?

* * * * * * *

They leaped out into space again, speeding along an arc that dropped them after two years into the atmosphere of another planet that had once, according to Matthew's memory and its interpretation of the charts, received a small group of Earthmen and their wives.

There was silence in the ship as it sank through cloud. No one dared to be optimistic.

The white veil parted, and they were moving with ponderous grace above a twisting river. The sharp crests of mountains reached up into the sky as though to trap the spaceship. The river cut its way down a valley and came out eventually on a plain of a dull red colour.

Clifford said: "A town—at the end of the valley."

They nosed down towards it. Red towers thrust up in noble patterns. In one area there had been a great deal of destruction, but the larger part of the town was intact. And above its roofs and pinnacles, darting to and fro like agitated bees, were swift helicars not unlike those that Matthew remembered.

"This is somewhere that hasn't been wiped out," he said, taking a deep breath. "Let's try making radio contact."

He sent out a signal of greeting. There was no response from the speaker on the panel. Again the message went out; and this time a spluttering and crackling burst from the speaker against their eardrums. It meant nothing. It was no more than blurred stuttering, with no resemblance to language or to any signalling system that Matthew knew.

"Must be vastly different equipment," he said. "Let's leave it open, though. We can set the transmitter to repeat, and maybe after a while they'll be able to adjust their sets to match up with ours."

The speaker continued to crackle as the ship made a slow circle and settled not far from the riverbank.

The bobbing, scurrying flyers above the town all seemed to converge on some special focal point, and then they disappeared.

Nothing moved outside, yet Matthew had a sense of being watched—of thousands of eyes watching the ship.

"They've emptied the streets," said Clifford. "We'd better get out and make friendly overtures before they all start screaming with fear like our last little acquaintance."

The chummering in the speaker swelled and grew more and more confused, as though on some adjoining wavelength messages were being hurriedly passed to and fro.

"Atmosphere check?" said Clifford, pushing himself out of his chair.

"Safe," said Matthew. "Slight surplus of oxygen. Don't get light-headed."

He followed Clifford along the corridor. Bellhouse emerged from the engine-room and said abruptly:

"Let me go. You and Clifford were first last time. You never know what risks there are: we ought to take it in turn,"

Matthew hesitated. Then he saw Clifford's eager face. His heart warmed to the younger man. The sense of adventure was still strong in Clifford. He wanted to be the first to set foot on this planet.

Matthew said: "I think we'll let Clifford make the preliminary exit. He's all set to go."

Clifford flashed him a smile of gratitude, and stepped into the airlock. Both doors opened wide, and there was a rush of sweet-smelling air that seemed to penetrate to the depths of the ship.

Matthew, framed in the opening, watched Clifford walk away from the ship and then turn back to wave.

As he did so, a helicar came streaking out from the city. It made a swift circle above the ship, and then darted back as though afraid of being snatched out of the sky if it lingered.

Clifford stood with his hands on his hips, surveying the towers and blocks of buildings that lay spread out before him.

Behind Matthew, Alida spoke urgently.

"Look—those things coming out of the town.... Call him back."

A group of helicars had formed above the roofline, and were skimming towards the ship.

"Official welcome delegation," said Matthew uncertainly.

Clifford looked up, and spread his arms to indicate

friendship.

Matthew suddenly called: "Clifford. Better come back. We're not sure. Don't take any chances."

The leading car, an angry droning little midge, swooped. Light stabbed like a bright lance from its side. There was a spurt of dust a few yards in front of Clifford, and then the ray struck him.

His arms were still outspread. They glowed for a fraction of a second. His body was outlined in flame. Then he crumpled and dissolved: where he had been there was a haze of dust, a swirl of movement that retained the shape of a man of a moment and then was dispersed.

Alida screamed. She would have flung herself past Matthew and out into the open, but he caught her arm and held her back.

"Bellhouse—the doors!" he shouted.

Bellhouse thumbed the switch, and the airlock door closed with a thud. As its echoes died away there was a sharp sound as though a great fingernail had scratched piercingly down the outside of the spaceship.

"It'll take more than that to pierce the hull," snapped Matthew.

The sound came again. Through the ports they saw the helicars swooping and plunging, sending out against the side of the ship a succession of vicious bright rays.

Alida was crying, her body racked by bitter sobs. Matthews' eyes narrowed with pain. He tried to put an arm about her shoulder, but she shook him off and showed him a face contorted by hatred.

"You!" she spat. "This is your fault. Your expedition to Earth...your selfishness...and it was you who let Clifford go out there."

He said: "Alida...."

"Where will it end? What hope is there now?"

Two of the women took her arms and led her gently away, trying to soothe her. The sound of her sobs came back with a hollow, resonant note as she went down the corridor.

Bellhouse said, not looking at Matthew: "Before we start any arguments, we ought to get clear of this place."

"Run away?" said Matthew, enraged. "We'll man the disruptors and blow those little insects out of existence."

"That's a fair-sized town over there," said Bellhouse, "and if I'm not mistaken they've got other resources. There's something moving over there now."

The two of them looked out of a port. Visibility was poor because of the columns of dust that lashed up out of the ground every time one of the helicar's rays swept across But Bellhouse was right. A vague shape of some heavy vehicle was moving into position at the end of one of the town's wide streets.

Matthew said; "We can stand up to it. We can give as good as we get."

"Can we? They'll be calling up reinforcements. They don't like the look of human beings—that's plain enough. And one hole blown in the side of the ship means we're stuck here until we can make repairs.

What's it going to be: do we clear out before we're damaged, or do we make a last stand?"

Matthew's every impulse was to stand fast. The need to avenge Clifford's death burned in his mind.

"Of course," said Bellhouse ironically, "we might be able to make them understand, after a while, that we mean no harm. But whether we'd get a chance of explaining is open to question."

The ground almost directly below the port burst into a fury of flame. The ship rocked violently, and Matthew was thrown back against the corridor wall.

Then another tremor ran through the ship, as the disruptors opened fire. Matthew thrust himself upright with a scowl of satisfaction.

Then he said, sharply: "You're right. Of course you're right. We can't expect to have a quiet talk with creatures who fire as soon as they see a human being, and we can't defeat them. It would be madness to come this far and then be wiped out because we were too proud to cut and run."

He called for one of the auxiliary pilots. Bellhouse went back into the engine-room. Matthew did not go to his usual seat, nor did he strap himself into position with the others in the lounge. He sent his rapid instructions booming through the ship, but he himself wrapped his arms around a corridor stanchion, and glared out of the window.

Another great blast of force struck at the ship. Matthew closed his eyes and cursed. Tears ran down his cheeks. He mouthed Clifford's name, and went on cursing bitterly until the roar of the take-off drowned out every sound, and pressure weighed on him so that everything went black and he hung limply by his arms from the stanchion.

Space claimed them again.

CHAPTER FIVE

Now they were conscious of nothing but a spirit of resignation. A sense of fatality settled on them all. Eternity stretched ahead of them, and eternity lay behind. They were rejected by the spinning worlds of the cosmos: they were doomed to wander out across the vastness of interstellar space with no hope, no promise of rest and contentment at last.

Alida was the only one who was not resigned. When she passed Matthew, her face glowed with hatred. If he tried to stop her and make her speak to him, she would wrench herself away and call him a murderer.

The others sank into sullenness. The years could roll on. There had never been such a place as Elysium, and there would be no such destination as Earth.

There were times when Matthew felt that he was too weak to go on any further with his weary odyssey. He sat at the control panel and was tempted to bring the whole thing to an end by hurling the ship out of its course and letting it spin madly off, like a stone from a catapult, into the furnace of some blazing sun.

At other times he merely wished that he would one morning not awaken. Let the end come for him, and for all of them, quietly. Call it a day. For him it had been a long day—a day composed of centuries.

They visited another world. It was dead. It had never lived. Lost in the cold, far from its sun, it showed no sign of ever having offered its bleak hospitality to any human being or other creature.

They left it and went on their way.

The men and women aged. The children grew up. Alida's beautiful face set into the sadness of maturity. She was marked by lines of suffering. There was only her daughter to give her comfort.

Eve was growing up into a beautiful girl. She had inherited all her mother's grace and strength of character. When Clifford had been alive, Matthew and Eve had spent a great deal of time together; but now Alida did all she could to keep them apart. She was not entirely successful. Eve had, as a little girl, conceived a deep affection for Matthew. He fascinated her and puzzled her.

"Why don't you grow older, like everybody else?" she once asked, putting her head on one side and studying him with her shrewd, observant eyes.

At first she laughed at his explanation and did not believe it. At some time in her life she must have learned that it was true, but it did not seem to affect her attitude towards Matthew in any way. She was neither afraid nor resentful.

However hard Alida might try to keep Matthew at a distance, the conditions in the ship made it impossible for her to live an entirely separate life with her daughter. Eve still smiled and talked to Matthew when they met. As she grew older, there was a deeper seriousness in her manner, but her affection did not seem to lessen.

The ship was becoming crowded by now. A number of children had been born in the course of the years. If any of the planets they had visited had been at all suitable, Matthew would have fallen in with the original suggestion that those who wished to stay behind and not complete the full journey should do so. But there had been nothing but the hostility of creatures who attacked automatically when they saw an Earthman, or else the bitterness of unfertile, dark worlds on which people bred in Elysium could never hope to live.

It was not until they were five years out from Earth that they discovered, on the last world they were to visit before they reached their destination, conditions like those of Elysium,

Here was the same mellow climate. Sparkling seas washed the gentle coasts of rich, luxuriant land.

"There must be a snag somewhere," said Bellhouse, an hour after the landing. "Someone is waiting somewhere with a flame-gun. Or else the nights are freezing and the plant life is deadly poison."

But the nights were warm. The plants and herbs made a feast, after years of living on Dr. Richard's shallow through sustaining cultures. Here was a replica of the comfortable world that they had left so far away in space and time. Here, at last, was comfort.

A dangerous comfort, thought Matthew.

Any enthusiasm the other members of the crew may

once have possessed for the voyage to Earth had faded long ago. Only doggedness and the obvious futility of trying to go back had kept them pressing on through space. Now they had found a planet which offered them tranquillity and rest. Why should they face another five years of wretchedness in the throbbing prison of the ship merely in order to reach a destination about which they knew nothing certain?

Matthew sensed this current of thought within a few days of landing. He was prepared to take the advantage of a month or two's holiday here before attempting the last lap. But he was not prepared to stay here forever.

Even Dr. Richard, who had been so reliable, was a member of the faction that wanted to stay. And that meant trouble. It was possible to leave half the members of the expedition behind if they wanted to settle here: the ship could still be handled by the remainder; but Dr. Richard, with his skill and the gift that was still known as 'green fingers', could not be spared.

"Life here is fascinating," said the biologist apologetic-ally. "There is so much here worth studying. It is a pity that we cannot stay. Living conditions are admirable."

"But it would be just as weak and unadventurous as staying on Elysium would have been," said Matthew. "We're so close to Earth. We can't give up now. One more journey—another five years—and we're there."

Dr. Richard pursed his lips. "Five years is not a great deal to you. To you it means little. But to some of us it means a great deal."

Matthew turned away. He saw that Alida was watching him, and for once her expression was not hostile. There seemed to be sympathy in it—pity, even. He was angry. He didn't want anybody's pity. He was immortal, and they well, look at them: their faces had aged, the young men were already well advanced into middle age, and some were prematurely old.

And they were lazy and unimaginative. All they wanted to do was settle down and live a dull, unambitious existence here, until some space raiders came along as the last lot had done and wiped out all their possessions.

He wondered if they had thought of that. Tackling Dr. Richard and a couple of the others about it, he said:

"Would you be happy living here, expecting an attack at any time? You have seen the other planets we've visited, and what happened to them. Why should you suppose this one will escape a similar fate, as soon as the murderers, whoever they were, find out that there's a colony here? And how do you know"—the thought struck him suddenly—"that there aren't already other people on another part of this planet, lying in wait for you?"

"We'd have seen them by now."

"Not necessarily."

The following day, spurred on by Matthew's disturbing suggestions, they took the ship up and made a survey of the planet. There was no sign of human life. Animals scuttered in alarm beneath the great shadow of the ship, but none of them appeared to be of a high level of intelligence, and there was no indication of any civilised community anywhere on the face of this world.

But three days later, in the mellow twilight that burnished the side of the spaceship to golden bronze, a man emerged from the woods and crossed the meadow in which the children were playing. He came with a hand oustretched in greeting. He was not one of the crew: he was a stranger.

Inside the ship, Matthew and Bellhouse interrogated him.

"How is it that we saw no sign of your colony when we flew over a few days ago?"

The newcomer, who had given his name as Diemer, smiled sadly.

"We have taken care to conceal ourselves whenever any unknown person or ship approaches. We have learned from experience."

"Experience?"

"You must have come from strange places," said Diemer curiously, "if you do not know what life has been like in the last twenty years or so."

"We have come from a long way away," said Matthew, determined to be noncommittal for the time being.

"It was plain that you were different from so many of our people. We watched your ship, and we came to study your encampment. And it was only when we saw that you were different, and sensed that you were not troublemakers, that I showed myself."

Matthew said: "What sort of trouble might we have been expected to make?"

"Where there are Earthmen, unfortunately, there is nothing but strife and bloodshed throughout the universe."

"We have come a long way," said Matthew again. "We've seen some terrible sights on our way. It's time we had an explanation. What has been happening?"

Diemer hesitated. He looked from one to the other as though weighing them up; then he reached a decision, and said: "I will tell you the whole story."

It was a story of steady conquest and exploitation. It was a story of greed and expansion—the old, vicious histories of national strife extended on to a cosmic scale.

The small colonies that had been left behind by the ship on which Matthew had made his outward journey had been largely involved. Growing larger, they worked with the natives of the planets on which they had landed, and eventually sent a small ship back to Earth or got in touch with Earth and directed new trading and emigration ships to the planets. The Earthmen were the pioneers of interplanetary travel. Holding the mastery of space, they held the mastery of commerce and scientific development. They picked the brains of the different peoples with whom they came in contact, and pooled the interplanetary resources for their own benefit.

Where the natives of different worlds objected to the domination of human beings, they were first coaxed and then, if necessary, threatened. There were massacres and outbreaks of cruelty. The wealth of the universe sent Earthmen mad: they took part in a rush beside which all the gold rushes and diamond booms of their own world paled into insignificance. The wider the bounds of the starry empire, the more grasping men became.

"There were liberal, humanitarian elements who disapproved," said Diemer, "but they fought a losing battle. When there are unlimited supplies of riches, and a civilisation is on the upgrade, it is always the brutal side of man that shows itself."

There were many Earthmen who were so filled with disgust at the savagery of their own people that they fled from Earth. They sought out unfertile planets, or at any rate planets that would not be seized by the acquisitive spaceships of the Interplanetary Development Bureau.

"The founders of our colony," said Diemer, "were among those who got away—in secrecy, with difficulty, leaving most of their belongings and cutting themselves away from a corrupt society."

"I don't know that I'd call this an unfertile planet," smiled Matthew.

"Not in the true sense of the word, perhaps. But to the Earthmen it wasn't of much use. There is no mineral wealth. The planet was explored in the early days of exploration, but there was no material here for the manufacture of atom blasts or the space torsion drive. It wasn't even positioned suitably for a supply station, or a jumping-off place for the patrol ships. It was just quiet, restful, and lonely. So they went on and left it. Their colonies were built up on more prosperous worlds."

But there was bound to be a day of reckoning. It took a long time for the downtrodden races of the universe to combine and muster the strength to oppose their conquerors. There were innumerable difficulties. The space patrols and all the power of Earth's commercial empire was widespread, and individual revolts were bound to fail. To attempt concerted action under the noses of human rulers was difficult and dangerous. But at last the great rebellion took place.

It was helped by a civil war that had broken out on Earth. The powers of the master planet fell out among themselves over the control of the universe, and in the course of their squabble had to recall many of their forces from the outposts of the universe. The races of the exploited planets seized their opportunity, combined, and overthrew the depleted armies and technical staffs that had been left to govern them.

Once started, there was no stopping the outbreak. Earthmen were slaughtered wherever they could be found. Generations of fear and hatred piled up behind the rebels: they had known oppression too long for them to be merciful and level-headed. With their own ships and the fast-moving ships captured from their governors, they ranged through the universe, launching attack after attack.

By the time the Earthmen had hastily settled their differences and turned to face the threat, it was too late.

The fanatical desire to claim freedom from the yoke of the Earthmen drove the rebels on and on, killing and laying waste. They did not hesitate to destroy their own cities when it was necessary to do so.

Great battles were fought out in space. Ships burned briefly, like the flickering of a candle flame against the brilliance of the stars. Planet after planet was ravaged. All the wealth and power of the universe was thrown away or destroyed in the furious conflict.

"Here on Platonia," said Diemer, "we hid ourselves. We had lived a simple life, free from hatred and greed, and we did not wish to be involved in the death throes of an evil system. Even now, when we believe that the war is ended and that few are left alive, we cannot take risks. If any of the rebels happen to visit this world and see us, they will kill us at once: Earthmen are killed at sight. And if Earthmen come, they are liable to kill us because we want no part of them, or to force us into the service of their shattered, defeated armies. Right and wrong have been submerged, forgotten. There has been nothing but killing. We consider it our duty to stay alive and build a small civilisation on finer foundations. I don't know if we shall succeed."

There was a long silence when he had finished. Outside the ship, the voices of children called brightly across the meadow. The sky was clear. The tale of war and destruction seemed remote and unreal.

At last Diemer spoke again. He said:

"Now tell me where you have come from. If all that I have told you is news to you, you must have come a great distance, from some forgotten world."

Bellhouse nodded to Matthew, who in his turn told the story of his immortality and the centuries he had spent in the far reaches of the universe. Diemer's eyes widened as he realised that this ship was the very one which had, in the distant past, left on various planets the people who eventually formed the nucleus of the Earth colonies.

"And now," he said, "what do you propose to do? You have spent a great time travelling. Where has it brought you?"

Bellhouse got up and looked through the port at the ground below, as though it would provide a satisfactory answer.

Matthew said slowly: "We still haven't reached the end of the journey. What is there...?" The words stuck in his throat. He had difficulty in speaking. "What," he asked at last, "is happening on Earth now? What shall we find when we get there?"

Diemer shook his head. "I don't know. We have had no message and no news from Earth for a long time. We know nothing of what has happened to it."

Now Matthew found himself facing the most strenuous opposition he had yet encountered. The voyagers, tired and middle-aged as most of them were, did not want to go any further. They had been told the story of the great war, and saw no reason for making the last jump to an Earth that might be completely ravaged. It could hold nothing that they wanted. Here on Platonia they could be content.

"But we must *know*," cried Matthew. "We must find out."

"What good will it do?" demanded Dr. Richard. "Life is too short. We might be killed as soon as we landed. There may be disease—death—great areas of radioactivity where battles have been fought. It would be reckless and without purpose to go on now."

There were murmurs of agreement. The rolling countryside of Platonia cast a spell on the travellers. They had had enough of the rigours of space.

The small colony of people hidden beyond the woods made them welcome. The boys who had grown up into young men in the space ship looked eagerly at the girl of their own age, who flatteringly considered them as magnificent adventurers. And Matthew noticed that the young men here were fascinated by Eve.

He stopped Alida one day and said to her: "Do you want your daughter to settle down here and marry one of those idle youngsters who has no imagination, no ambition and no knowledge of anything but his own little world?"

"What else have you to offer her?" asked Alida coldly. "Have you anything better?"

He could not answer.

Already his companions were building small huts, roofed with the large trailing vines and timbers of the luxuriant woodland. Concealed as the homes of the colonists were concealed, they made a small, happy village in the shade of the great trees.

"You may as well face it," said Dr. Richard, rather

shamefacedly. "The expedition is at an end."

But Matthew was not prepared to give up. He lashed them with his tongue. They stared at him sullenly. If only he would be quiet, they would be perfectly content. If only he were not here: that was the thought that ran through their minds, he knew.

As a matter of principle he stayed on board ship instead of building himself a home outside. Quite apart from anything else, he distrusted them. There had been mutterings about wrecking the ship so that there should be no question of it carrying them any further. And the original colonists were not too pleased: they said that it was too noticeable and that it might draw the attention of any visitor to the planet.

"If that's how your people really feel," said Matthew sharply to Diemer, "they'd better help me to persuade my lot to embark as soon as possible."

"We do not wish to interfere. We have tried to keep strife and dissension out of our society. Any decisions you make will have to be free decisions. We would like your ship out of the way; but we leave it to you to decide how that is to be done. You may go with it on your journey to Earth; or you may destroy it."

"Destroy it?"

The threat was always there now. He was so close to home—to Earth—and yet there was every chance, that he might never reach it. There need only be a swift action on the part of his dissatisfied colleagues, and the ship would be crippled.

One night he awoke in darkness, certain there had

been some unusual sound in the resonant corridors and empty cabins. He lay absolutely still. It came again—a shuffling of feet and the faintest murmur of voices. He swung himself silently down from his bunk and crossed the room.

Before he could reach the flame gun that lay beside his chair, the door was flung open. Three men came in quickly, snapping on the lights.

Matthew tackled the first one without waiting to ask questions. But the other two fell on him and dragged him away, twisting his arms back and fastening them behind his back with a swift efficiency that showed they had planned every move of this attack.

He was forced down into his chair. The tallest of the three—Matthew's old opponent, who had once before revolted when they were out in space—reached for the flame gun and toyed with it menacingly. He said:

"We're going to put paid to the controls of this ship."

Matthew writhed forward. "You can't do it. It—"

He was pushed back.

"Why can't you see reason? We don't want to make trouble, but you're a menace. We've got to finish this ship off so that the idea of going on to Earth is scrapped once and for all. And if we have to finish you off as well, then that'll be done."

Matthew saw that they meant it. They were pale, but quite decided. He said, not asking for pity but driving the point angrily home:

"You know what this will mean? After coming all this distance—"

"We know that it's a disappointment for you, but there are others to consider. As long as you're around and the ship intact, you'll give none of us any peace. And what we want now is peace. We've had enough. We've come far enough with you."

Matthew said: "You seem worried about my influence. If everyone feels as you do, why bother if I keep talking? Are you afraid of me?"

"You're a nuisance. You might talk some of them round...."

"Ah! That's it!" cried Matthew triumphantly. "You know that plenty of them feel ashamed of not going right on to the end. They're wavering, but if I keep on at them they'll come with me to Earth. That's it, isn't it?"

"You've no right to influence them. You've got to be silenced."

"You'll never silence me."

The flame gun came up and pointed steadily at his chest. "We've had enough arguments. You're going to be silenced, even if it means killing you."

And then a voice said: "There will be no killing."

Diemer and three of his men came briskly into the room, with Eve hurrying behind them. She gave a gasp of relief when she saw Matthew.

The flame gun was wrenched from the man's grasp. He said: "What right have you—?"

"There has been enough killing. There has been too much murder and hatred in the universe. Here on Platonia we will have no bloodshed."

"This man is inhuman. He's lived too long. He has no right to play with the destinies of short-lived human beings merely in order to satisfy his whims."

Diemer said gravely: "He has the right to try to convince people. Tomorrow we must have a decision. Tomorrow the whole matter must be discussed."

Eve was freeing Matthew's hands. He felt the touch of her slim fingers on his skin, and looked up at her in wonderment. She smiled shakily. He felt a great surge of hope, mingled with downright disbelief, when he saw the expression in her eyes.

She said: "I guessed what they were up to. I warned Diemer."

"I didn't realise you were as...as interested," he said lamely.

Again she smiled. "We shall reach Earth," she said.

* * * * * * *

The next day there was a meeting attended by all the passengers of the ship and a large number of the Platonians. Matthew spoke fervently of the need to get to Earth and find out what had happened. He spoke of their ancestry, of Earth as the mother of all the people who had spread out across the universe.

"Admittedly," he said frankly, "the results of that expansion have been terrible. We cannot be proud of what our race has done. But is that any excuse for giving up our quest and settling down to a placid life in these surroundings? We said we would make the journey to Earth. We accepted a challenge. Are you going to give up now? If comfort is going to come before the sense of adventure, the human race is certainly doomed—and despite everything bad that has happened, I believe the human race should still strive and take risks, and ask questions."

He tried to put across to them his own conviction of the cosmic importance of this return to Earth. It was difficult. To them it was only a name. They had not been the pioneers: they were not going home.

But suddenly Eve jumped up and stood beside him. She cried: "What's wrong with everybody? Are you all afraid to face what may be waiting on Earth? It's not just laziness and the desire for comfort that's keeping you here: it's cowardice. I've never seen Earth, and I've never seen Elysium. I know which is the nearer now, and I want to get there. I don't want to die of boredom. At least while we were in the ship we were travelling—we were going somewhere, and wondering what it would be like. If we settle down here there will be no wonder left. We'll know everything that is ever likely to happen to us. I want to strike out into the unknown—to ask questions and find the answers, and still keep asking questions...."

She lashed them with her youthful, impetuous fury. Matthew listened, his mind in a turmoil. At one moment he caught her mother's eye. Alida was staring at him, something also like fear in her eyes; and then there was compassion and a strange resignation in the place of fear.

The arguments were over. Some of the men and

women would stay, but several of them, including Dr. Richard, would carry on to the end of the journey. And there were actually some volunteers from Platonia. Several of the young men and women, and one or two middle-aged people, joined the crew.

There were enough of them to take the ship safely to Earth.

Matthew caught Eve's hand and held it. They both laughed wildly, foolishly.

Alida came up to them. She said to Matthew: "I shall come, too. Clifford would have wanted it. My daughter is quite right, and I'm proud of her. I want to see this journey through to the end."

CHAPTER SIX

They were all five years older. Perhaps some of them regretted the decision they had taken. Perhaps they dreamed sometimes of the Platonian tranquillity just as, earlier, the original members of the crew had dreamed of Elysium. But they had come, and here they were in the spaceship as it spun down at last through the solar system that Matthew remembered.

He was very silent. There was no exultation in his mind: only a numbness that made it impossible for him to describe his feelings, even to himself.

The sun glowed in familiar skies. The pattern of stars was one that he remembered from a distant past that suddenly seemed very close.

Eve stood by him in the control room. Every now and then she asked some question and he responded automatically. He did not let himself think of Eve too much. She was beautiful now, and he was afraid of her beauty. He wanted her as he had never wanted any woman before: but at the back of his mind was the knowledge that she would grow old while he stayed unnaturally young. For her sake he would not let her go through that experience.

The ship quivered with the thrust of its retarding blasts. Slowly it entered Earth's atmosphere.

Now Matthew was to be put to the test. He sat rigid, afraid of what they would find. He had driven these people on: he had urged them to come with him, to keep travelling until they reached the home of their ancestors; and what would they find?

It was as though Eve read his thoughts. She put her hand lightly on his shoulder.

"Whatever happens," she said, "it's been a great adventure. It had to be undertaken."

He would have liked to show how grateful he was for her calm reassurance, but there was nothing he could say or do. Automatically he issued instructions to his young co-pilot, one of the Platonians who had passed five interested years learning all that the ship could teach him.

Clouds writhed about the ship and then were gone.

Abruptly, emerging like a picture that had come unexpectedly into focus, the Earth was below them, clear and bathed in sunlight.

Matthew said tensely: "All right. I'll take over."

He recognised the area of the North American coastline, above which they had come out. And he knew that the huddled ruins some miles to the south must represent what had once been New York.

Ruins....

For two days and nights he kept the ship on a zigzag, twisting course above the Earth. He refused to pass the controls over to any of the other pilots. Desperately, racing through hours of darkness into the sunlight of another day, he sought for a sign of hope. But cities were already being overrun by grass and weeds. Nature was reclaiming its old territories. In South America the jungles had marched back upon man's civilisation. In the North, where once had been the great industrial and experimental area of White Sands City, there were only gaping craters, a bleak desert that looked like the surface of the moon.

Across Asia and Europe—above places whose names were now only a memory: and, thought Matthew, those names existed only in his memory. There was nobody else alive who had known them. All that was left of human civilisation on Earth was locked in his mind.

His eyes were red with weariness. Not just the weariness of this grim exploration, but the fatigue of centuries. He was conscious of the loss of friends across the years. One after another they had died, while he went on living. And now he looked down on the remains of what had once been his world. There was nothing left. There was only himself, utterly alone. The people in the spaceship were not really his people. They were strangers.

"Matthew...."

Eve was talking to him. She was saying that he must rest. She was trying to persuade him to bring the ship down, to sleep and be quiet for a time until his energies were restored. He heard the words, but their meaning did not come over to him.

The last place he meant to visit was not far away. He had half-deliberately slowed the ship, as though afraid to find this last proof of despair. But the English Channel gleamed below, and the shadow of the ship moved across it like a dark stain.

There, at last, was London. The white belt of skyscrapers that had encircled the old city had fallen. From here the circle of buildings that had been conceived and constructed in Matthew's youth looked like nothing so much as a ring of white ash. And within the circle lay what was left of the ancient metropolis. The dome of St. Paul's, cracked like an eggshell, still stood up above the surrounding desolation, but most of the body of the building had crumbled. The dome itself would not stand up much longer. It was a memorial to vanished splendour, and soon it would collapse and lie defeated with the rest of the city.

The spaceship veered in a dizzy arc, and began to lose height.

Eve cried out. The co-pilot tried to wrench Matthew's hands from the controls, but Matthew held on firmly without knowing what he was doing. A wave of darkness rolled up over his vision. He could no longer see. Tiredness and dizziness closed on him, yet through the haze he was aware of voices, and of a woman screaming down the echoing corridors of the ship.

At the last moment he opened his eyes. Beyond the observation port a slanting green wall was racing up to meet them. A strip of sea glanced along a crazily tilted horizon.

Then there was an impact that smashed Matthew forward against the control panel. The enclosed world of the ship was filled with a great explosion of noise, a splintering and a scream of shattered engines.

And then silence.

* * * * * * *

He awoke to pain. His head and his right shoulders throbbed with deep agony. He felt sick inside, as though his stomach had been pounded viciously.

Light struck at his eyes and he turned his head. At once it was pain again, so swift that he almost fell again into unconsciousness. Very slowly he opened his eyes, carefully not moving his head.

Eve said: "You're all right. You're going to be all right."

He was lying on a smooth stretch of grass, through which a faint wind whispered fretfully. Above him the sky seemed monstrous, a great curve over this expanse of flat land.

"Don't try to sit up."

"The others?" he asked weakly. "Everybody else— what happened to them?"

"Nobody killed," she said soothingly. "A few broken

legs and arms. But it could have been worse. Much worse. We drove into the mud at the side of a ditch—we went in a long way. There was nobody in the nose of the ship, so things weren't too bad."

"And the ship?"

He knew the answer without being told. The ship had come off lightly, but it was certainly damaged: and how, on a forsaken world, could that damage ever be repaired?

Bellhouse loomed above him, looking down with a twisted yet affectionate smile. He said: "Well, Matthew, we made it. We're here. This is the end of the trip."

"The end? Yes," said Matthew dully, "this is the end."

It was some time before he was steady enough to walk any distance. Bellhouse supervised the unloading of stores, ready for a long stay.

"Somehow," he said to Matthew a few days later, "I don't think we'll be making any more journeys."

They sat in the musty-smelling living room of an old farmhouse. There were holes in the roof, but this ancient building had stood up to the ravages of time better than most of the modem edifices they had seen. The main building and its outhouses served as a temporary headquarters.

Behind the house was the gentle slope of a hill, at the top of which was another deserted house that could easily be taken over and repaired. Before them was the stretch of coastal plain that ended in a ridge of sand dunes. A warm breeze blew persistently off the sea, rustling without ceasing in the reeds and tall grasses that rose from the dykes and streams that made a complicated pattern over the plain. Here and there, along a ridge that stood above the level expanse, ran old forgotten roads, some of them no doubt dating back to the twentieth and twenty-first centuries.

Matthew said: "It certainly looks as though we won't be able to take off for a long time. To repair that ship here will be even more difficult than it was to get it into shape on Elysium."

"We've got to make the best of things," said Bellhouse coolly. "Here we are on Earth, and that's that."

They watched Eve walking towards the farmhouse. She had been strolling across the fields, weaving her way in and out of the network of ditches, and bending over the wild flowers that sprang up from the banks. The eyes of the two men followed her, although they went on talking abstractedly.

Matthew said: "I suppose there's a great deal of resentment? I mean, now that they've seen what Earth is like, most of them will want to get back to Platonia, and it's my fault that they can't do it."

Bellhouse shook his head thoughtfully. "No," he said. "No, I don't believe it's like that at all. They're all interested. I don't know what there is about the place but...well, now that we're here, we've got a sort of feeling that it's an important place. Our ancestors started out from here, and we've come back. The human race hasn't been entirely wiped out from the face of the Earth. Not yet."

"It's good to hear you say that. I hadn't expected quite such a reaction. It...it means a lot to me."

Bellhouse got up from the old wooden chair on which he had been sitting.

"Nobody's despondent," he said. "Some of the youngsters want to set out and explore the country. They think there must be somebody living, somewhere. And even if there isn't, they want to—to—"

"To see the world?" said Matthew with a laugh.

"More or less."

"There may be some Inuits," said Matthew wildly. "Or even some people hiding out in the Welsh mountains. And even in the ruins of London: you never can tell."

"There are thousands of things we have to find out," said Bellhouse. "There must be records to be unearthed. One or two of us want to go to London and see what we can discover. Buried under all that rubble there must be books or visual records of events over the past centuries. We've got a lot to learn—a lot of history to reconstruct for ourselves."

"Do you think you will really learn anything from it?"

"If we're ever going to make an attempt to rebuild—"

"To rebuild without mistakes?" said Matthew. "To start from the beginning, only making sure that this time there are no wars and no errors? It's quite a task."

"It's one worth tackling."

Eve came into the room, her face flushed and a new freedom in her movements.

She said: "To be able to walk straight ahead for miles and miles if you want to, instead of turning round at the end of a metal corridor and pacing back again! It's wonderful."

Bellhouse glanced at her and then at Matthew. He smiled slightly, and made some brief remark about going to see about the dismantling of some of the ship's equipment.

When he had gone, Eve came and stood by Matthew's chair.

"It's a fascinating world," she said. "Life is exciting."

"There's nothing like it," he agreed sardonically.

She looked about the room, and nodded approval. "It could be nice here," she said. Then, with a strange uncertainty in her voice, she went on. "What are you going to do now? Do you want to go with the London investigation group, or with the travellers? Or have you some other idea?"

"I don't know what I want," said Matthew. "I simply don't know. I feel terribly tired. Nothing seems to mean anything any more."

He looked up into her face. Her lips were parted. He could not help himself. He reached up for her, and a stab of pain lanced through his arm, but he paid no heed to it: he had his arm round her, and she was bending over him and he was kissing her.

"Matthew," she said gently as she drew away. "Matthew, this is a time for new beginnings, for—"

"No." He snapped the word out abruptly. He turned away from her and stared resolutely out of the window.

"No, it wouldn't do. I ought not to have...oughtn't to have made a fool of myself."

"I've been waiting for you to do that for a long time."

He said, as curtly as possible: "I have lived for several hundred years, and I am likely to live for several hundred more. Do you want to grow old while I go on wearing this smirking, ridiculous young face? I've caused too much unhappiness already. I couldn't bear to bring you any pain for the sake of a brief happiness—"

"For me," she said, "it wouldn't be brief. For me it would be my lifetime."

"But—"

"And I shall be content," she said resolutely, "if I think that, two hundred years from now, I am nothing more than a memory in your mind—just one memory among thousands. That will be enough for me."

She was proof against all his arguments. Her faith and love shone from her eyes. He felt humble, and was at the same time filled with an incredible hopefulness.

Eve said: "It will take hundreds of years—thousands, perhaps—before this planet is thickly populated again. It may become a menace to the universe once more, or it may become a world of enlightenment and reason. A lot depends on us. I'd like us to start out together. Not in any big way," she added breathlessly: "The beginnings ought to be here, on this farm. Let the others explore and found new colonies, or dig up ancient records and piece the bits together. We'll live here. If you want to, of course. If you want to go away,

I'll come with you."

He shook his head. The world framed in the window shone green and promising in the sunlight. He said:

"If I go away, it will be afterwards. A long time from now. For the time being I want to stay here. There may be trouble. There may be invaders from other worlds. We may not have long to live. I don't know. But we must carry on as though the future were assured, and in our own hands. Once I killed a man on this Earth. It was in a struggle, and I did not want to kill him. But because of me and my greed for immortality he died. If I can make some restitution by starting all over again on this same Earth...."

She grasped his hand. There was no more to be said. He knew that it was settled between them.

Her mother, Alida, gave Matthew a sad smile when the news was broken to her. But there was something besides sadness in it. She said:

"I think this is right, Matthew. You have suffered a great deal. I believe this is right, and I hope it brings you both happiness."

A small group took over the farmhouse and its neighbour on the hillside. The other two groups set off on their journeys, one to London and the other into the unknown reaches of the country. They were all possessed by a mood of confidence and eagerness.

To Matthew it was as though the past had been wiped out. He did not let himself consider the burden of years that still lay ahead. He worked in the fields and came home tired and happy to his wife Eve. They worked on the renovation of the farmhouse and on the provision of crude furniture. As their skills improved, they replaced the original crudities with more accomplished work.

Eve bore two sons, and sparkled with health and a vivacity that never failed to thrill Matthew. It was only after the birth of the second one that he had a fit of depression; he visualised his two sons growing old—passing him on the road of life, aging before his eyes.

With determination he shook off this mood, and went on working.

Two of the London party came back at the end of a year with news of the records they had unearthed, and after that first visit a regular contact was maintained. At the end of six years the small farming community was startled by the appearance of a well-constructed coach drawn by two horses.

"Progress!" laughed Bellhouse as he shook Matthew's hand. "There's no telling what we'll think of next!"

They went into the house laughing, but in the doorway Bellhouse paused. He gave a puzzled frown.

"What's the matter?" asked Matthew.

Bellhouse was staring at him. He said uncertainly: "You look older, Matthew. You've got a couple of grey hairs."

Eve, coming across the room to greet him, caught her breath. She said: "Yes. I know he has. But I never thought.... I've kept all thoughts about that sort of thing at the back of my mind, and somehow I just took the grey hairs for granted, and...."

She was crying and laughing at the same time.

Matthew strode past her and looked in the polished copper surface of the large pan over the fireplace. It told him nothing clearly. But were there lines under his eyes—faint lines, such as would be normal for a man who was no longer in his twenties but had passed on into the thirties.

"It's impossible to be sure," he said. "You can't tell. It may mean nothing. It'll be a year or two before we can suppose anything's really happening."

But they had not been mistaken. As the years went by, Matthew aged. He remembered what Philipson had said so long ago. "We may one day find planets on which the optimum conditions prevail. There will be none of the physical friction. On such a planet, a man who had been injected with this culture might be almost immortal. Only if he came back to Earth would he once more start—though slowly—to wear away." Elysium had been the planet with ideal conditions. There, Matthew bad been an immortal. But he had come home to Earth, and the shock to his metabolism had evidently jarred him into the ordinary time stream of human existence once more.

Perhaps centuries ago he would have been afraid. Like any other mortal, he was now faced with death at the enc of a short life. But instead of fear, he felt a great rush of thankfulness.

It was a new life. All the past was cancelled out. The winds and the sunshine and the beauty of the world acquired a meaning. He would not be here to enjoy them forever, and that fact gave them far more splendour than they had possessed before.

"I shall live out my life like any other man," he said aloud, "and I shall grow old as my wife grows old, and at the end of it I shall die."

It was simple yet magnificent. It was more wonderful than any promises of immortality had ever been.

And in Eve's bright face he found the confirmation that this was the right and true existence, and that whatever happened now, their happiness was assured.

THE RECUSANTS

Of course I understand how Henning and Myrna came to spurn the regime of the Newmen. Who should have a better knowledge than I of the workings of their minds?

Henning was the son of a couple who had married quite young, which probably accounts for the failure of the Newmen conditioning to 'take' as securely as it ought to have done. He inherited too many memories and too much youthful intransigence from his father—a reactionary who had never thoroughly assimilated the teachings of the pioneer Newmen. Henning's father did not propose to submit to his children: he would not accept wisdom from them; and the stubborn hostility he thus implanted in his son's mind was bound to set up a conflict there.

No doubt the problem lay dormant during the early years. But when Henning married Myrna, they had to face up to it

Myrna said: "When we have children...."

She was small and dark, with a smooth olive skin and deep, wistful eyes. He was taller, and had a slight stoop—he gave the appearance of always bending protectively over her.

"When we have children, what shall we do? We must decide."

The two of them were sitting in their three-roomed apartment overlooking the Thames. Henning had just pulsed a helicar, and they had two minutes to wait before they were taken out to dinner with friends. The thought of those friends was preying on them—they knew what to expect.

"The pattern for us," said Henning, with distaste, "will be the same as the pattern for Paul and Lucille Marsh. Or for anyone else."

"We've got to decide," said Myrna. "There must be a way. We must be able to choose."

"As long as we live here, under the radiation blanket, we shall produce a child who will be our ruler."

Myrna got up and went to the door leading to the next room. In there, according to the architect's design and also according to law, was to be a nursery. She looked at the bare walls on which their first child would tell them what pictures to hang; at the bare shelves, for which he or she would order chosen micro-recordings at the built-in cot with its adjacent control knobs for remote operation of the telescreen and audio amplifier.

And she said: "You do want us to get out, don't you Henning? Truly?"

"Yes," he said. "Before it's too late. Before you have a child."

Her small red lips were pursed. Her strangely defenceless little face was pale and wry with wonderment.

"It's odd that we should have met and married two people as difficult as we are. The chances against our meeting...."

"If I hadn't met you," he said with a warmth that brought the colour gratefully back to her cheeks, "I should never have married at all. It's only because—"

The helicar buzzed its signal from the roof, and they went up ten storeys to the exit.

* * * * * * *

The trip was a short one. The car lifted them above London and turned north towards the residential blocks of St. Albans. Traffic was brisk at this time of the evening, but it was only a matter of moments before they swung off Skyway Beam A5 and dropped to the gleaming white estate below.

Paul and Lucille Marsh were waiting for them on the roof.

"So nice you could come," said Lucille.

They shook hands and smiled bright, conventional smiles.

Myrna said: "What a lovely evening, isn't it?"

"Is it?"

The Marshes, taken by surprise, stared up into the sky. The retreating helicar was, for a moment, an iridescent blob of silver against a rolling wave of cumulus, tinged with fading crimson. Paul Marsh looked puzzled. Myrna realized that she had embarrassed him—the Marshes were responsible, middle-aged citizens who did not make a point of gazing into the evanescent phenomena of the skies.

Paul said: "Well, let's go in, shall we?"

The apartment was slightly larger than the one in which Henning and Myrna lived; but its essential features were the same: People today, after all, wanted more or less the same things. More spacious accommodation was a sign of a mounting age group and increased responsibility, but there was no reason for any eccentric variation in the main equipment. There was, however, one big difference here. The nursery was occupied.

"Rowena," said Lucille proudly, "is going to order the dinner."

Henning glanced surreptitiously at Myrna. They were both taut, trying to look polite and respectful—and finding it hard going.

Their hosts seemed unaware of the tension. There was pride in Paul's face as his wife went into the nursery; pride that glowed even more strongly when she returned, leading by the hand a two-year-old girl. Only it wasn't quite that thought Henning with a shiver of distaste (I can feel that shiver of distaste now)—the child, not the mother, was the one in control—the child was, incongruously, the senior.

"Hello, Rowena," said her father, his greying head turned towards her as though waiting for her slightest command.

Her wide eyes turned a cool, appraising stare up to him, and then glanced at the visitors. Her shrewd gaze focused on Henning.

She said: "Good evening. I understand from Paul that you work in his office."

"That's right," said Henning stiffly.

"We must have a talk one day. I've thought of several ways of reorganizing the electronic computer bankings."

"She doesn't waste any time, does she?" said Paul with a deferential smile.

Rowena's brief glance in his direction was a mingling of tolerance and contempt. She sensed, as one could hardly fail to do, the confusion in his mind—the instinctive parental affection jarring with the awed realisation that the child represented a more advanced stage of human development and would soon be in legal charge of the household. Yes, Rowena understood; but there was no more than a formal pity in her understanding. She was already too far advanced to be capable of emotional states such as that of sympathy.

She withdrew her hand from her mother's, and moved towards the kitchen dial panel. Her small, stubby fingers began to prod and punch decisively.

* * * * * * *

The food was splendid. There were combinations and piquant clashes of flavours such as Henning had never before imagined.

And it was a relief to find that there were only four of them at table.

Nevertheless, Myrna felt compelled to say: "What a

pity Rowena couldn't stay up to enjoy the dinner she's ordered."

Lucille smiled. "The fact that she is mentally so advanced doesn't mean that she is physically capable of our sort of living yet," she said. "She has a flair for taste patterns, but her stomach needs to be older before it's allowed to deal with such things at this time of day. Rowena herself would be the first to insist on our adhering to the regulations."

"It seems so odd."

"Odd?"

"This...well, this business of being dominated by a child who can only just toddle—who has to go to bed early, whose stomach isn't ready yet for large meals in the evening...." Myrna's voice tailed away as she realised how shocked Lucille looked.

Paul laughed bluffly. "It'll all sort itself out when you have a child of your own. Not that that'll happen for some years yet, eh?" he added.

"Why not?" Myrna blurted out. "Henning and I would like to have children soon—while we're still young."

Paul tried to preserve his bluff manner, but it was shot through with uneasiness. He lowered his voice, as though fearful that Rowena might be listening at the bedroom door.

"That's not advisable, you know," he murmured. "Not advisable at all."

His wife nodded confirmation. She licked her lips, nodded again, and said: "You don't give the baby a chance. You and Henning need to mature before transmitting your knowledge to your child." The words came out swiftly and mechanically, like a well-learnt lesson. "The longer you wait, the finer the inheritance for your child."

"Yes, but...."

Myrna caught Henning's eye, and stopped.

For the rest of the evening, conversation was general. Henning warily avoided provocative topics. Paul Marsh was his boss—you didn't argue with your boss, or let your wife argue with your boss.

Particularly about the principles of the Newmen.

Now that he had met Rowena, Henning found that there were questions in his mind. Questions he could not ask. He could not ask Paul Marsh how soon it would be before control of the research wing passed into the hands of that small girl sleeping in that next room. He could not ask whether, when Paul had to take a back seat, there would be other changes, new instructions.

So they talked about the new pulsator, which had simplified interplanetary transmissions, and about the daily office and laboratory routine from which one might have thought they would have been glad to escape. It was all safe and unprovocative.

Even so, Lucille could not help bringing Rowena's name in at intervals. Her mind went back to her over and over again. The household revolved around the child. And even when Paul did not mention her by name, the thought of her was clearly there.

Rowena, it leaked out, had conceived a wonderful

idea for a much larger telescreen projection without having to buy the commercial equipment. So simple, yet so brilliant. Rowena had taken a vague promotion scheme of her father's, and developed an entirely new angle on it. Rowena had combined her mother's and father's ideas on redecoration of the flat, and come up with a splendid new scheme.

Rowena....

Lucille hummed as she lifted the table flap and pressed it against the wall for the plates to be discharged into the disposal chute. And she turned and said:

"That tune...Rowena remembered it for me. Did I tell you, Paul?"

"No," said Paul.

"She must have taken it over from me, along with everything else. I'd forgotten all about it—such a pretty tune, I used to love it—and suddenly she started singing it this morning. To be able to pull that up out of my memory—only of course it's her memory now—isn't it wonderful?"

Yes, wonderful.

I know that even Henning and Myrna, in revolt as they were against the whole regime of the Newmen, nevertheless thought it was wonderful.

And loathsome.

They were early Newmen themselves, but they had been produced by parents who resented the existence of the radiation blanket. They had not been allowed to dominate their homes; their fathers had angrily condemned those early experiments and their gradual introduction into the life of the country and then of the world.

The original experiments had been greeted by many other people with hostility—but by a great many more with incredulity. There had been shouts of derision. Television comedians in every country built a succession of jokes round the idea. New reporters went looking for new variations on the story, new gimmicks, new details of freaks and freakish happenings.

KIDS TO RULE THE ROOST, boomed the headlines. ORDERS FROM THE CRADLE.... JUNIOR FOR PRESIDENT.... NO SECRETS FROM BABY....

Jokes about mothers-in-law were swiftly converted into extravagant and improbable jokes about daughters-in-law—aged two and under.

But scorn was no weapon against reality. The Newmen had arrived.

The experiments continued, the children were born, and gradually those parents who had refused treatment began to realize that their own nice, ordinary children were going to be left behind in life's struggle. A baby who inherited his mother's and father's combined memories—with all the technical and practical knowledge and skills of both parents, plus a clear picture of their emotional relationships and problems—stood a better chance of getting on in the world than did an ordinary child whose education was spread over the first twenty years of life. Formal schooling could not give a quarter of what was given to Newmen babies at the moment of birth, and before.

As more generations came along, the variation would be more and more marked. Grandchildren and great-grandchildren would be born with even more comprehensive knowledge. Their intellects would be the sum of all those preceding intellects, which had blended into their own.

The protests began to change their tune. Those who had howled most loudly against this impious tampering with nature began to howl with equal force for similar treatment for themselves. They didn't intend to see their children overhauled and left behind by the children of others. Democracy demanded an inheritance of brilliance for all, not for a chosen few, whose brainpower would soon put them in a position to rule the world and outwit any opponents.

"But this is a complex process," the technicians protested. "Individual results can be guaranteed. The difficulties in mass application...."

They might as well have advocated the view that automobiles should all be hand-made, for the benefit of a select few.

"Find a way," said the governments of the world, harassed by their peoples.

The scientists reconsidered their original findings, and took steps to find a way.

The fact that it was possible to transmit the entire contents of a human mind into the embryo mind of a child not yet born had been discovered during investigations into the reactions of dogs to atomic motors. It had been noticed very early in the days of atomic-powered vehicles, that dogs were seriously disturbed by them. Radiations not perceptible to humans—and, apparently, in no way harmful—were emitted by the new motors, and these had the same effect on certain animals as a painful supersonic vibration might have. Research was instituted at once; and after a series of tests on various theories, it was found that a development of these same radiations could produce remarkable effects in human children.

An intermittent pulse injected into the brain awoke certain activities in the cortex that had been unknown before. Hitherto unused areas of the brain awoke and set to work—secretly, almost surreptitiously, it seemed to the pioneer research workers. It was only when the first Newmen children were born that the full significance of this mental activity became apparent.

An old dream of philosophers came true. Language, knowledge, experience...all were transmissible. Even personal memories could be handed on intact, in their full vividness. No longer need every child go through the laborious business of starting its education with the simple banalities, the essential but primitive groundwork—no longer was there the wearisome shaping of disjointed sounds into speech; no longer the groping for comprehension of words, concepts, diagrams, numerals. The child began where its parents left off. The child of a philosopher or scientist took up the threads of the father's work and went on without flagging.

Human progress would be incalculably speeded up.

The portents were all there. Given a few generations, mankind would increase its stature a hundredfold—a thousandfold.

The new process was speedily evolved. At other times, in other circumstances, its development might have taken considerably longer. But now there was the advice of the children to be acted on—the shrewd, mature, analytical children in the vanguard of the Newmen. They could tackle a problem of this sort with greater competence than their parents at a similar age could have tackled the building of a column of wooden blocks.

Blanket radiation was the swiftly-devised solution. A layer of force was generated over every major city and town. Beneath it, basking in it as in the radiance of an invisible sun that gave off no heat, men and women lived their normal lives. They worked, played, married...and brought into the world babies who knew their innermost thoughts and combined their talents.

The old order changed.

Physical limitations were all that held these new beings in check. For the formative years—and now 'formative' referred only to the development of physique—they had to depend on their parents to carry out their wishes. Adult in mind at birth, and adult in speech within the first twelve months of life, the children gave the orders. The whole balance of society shifted. Parental responsibility, so much talked about at every period of human evolution, changed its character—instead of being the responsibility of grown people towards their immature, defenceless children, it became the responsibility of inferiors towards their betters. Laws were soon put into effect, framed by two-year-olds, whereby property was automatically transferred from parents to their first-born child, with a complicated but efficient scale of adjustments if other children were born later.

In point of fact, very few parents had more than one child. The decline in the birth rate was even more noticeable in the second and third generations. The first-born child, particularly when this was a son, tended to make such intensive use of its parents and to overawe them so swiftly, that they were unable to contemplate the presence of another child in the household. Then again, the fast-developing minds of the Newmen soon grappled with world problems—with famine, disease, and overcrowding—and saw that the logical step was to reduce the population of Earth as soon as possible. Large families were anti-social. With world peace in sight, the old need for large families as cannon fodder was no longer a valid argument.

But still the world was not entirely populated with Newmen. There were still others.

Outside the cities there were still, in places, children who were no more than children. And there were reactionaries who went to join the exiles.

* * * * * * *

Myrna said: "That settles it."

"I think it does," agreed Henning.

They were being carried away from the Marsh home in a helicar, drifting smoothly over the gleaming lights of the widespread city. It was a tranquil night; a radiant, glorious night—for those with eyes to see.

"I couldn't face it," said Myrna. "I couldn't bear to see contempt in the eyes of any child of mine. I want to be a mother, not a slave."

"They'll say we're selfish," said Henning. "That's what they say about anyone who break away from the pattern. They'll say we can't sink our selfish pride and realize that it is all for the good of the race."

"Let them say. But they won't stop us."

"There's no law to prevent our leaving the community. It's just that we're...well...."

"Social outcasts?" she smiled.

"Sort of."

They dipped gently towards their roof. The glowing city rose up about them. A million sparkling eyes swam over and around them.

Myrna said: "I can't say I'm very worried."

"If you're sure—"

"I'm sure. Quite sure. You know we wouldn't be happy here."

They went down to their flat. The door opened before Henning's fingers, a gentle light came on automatically. He put his hand on Myrna's arm. They looked towards the nursery door, which she had left open. The bareness of the room seemed to draw them towards it—the suction of a vacuum.

Myrna stared in once more, and shivered.

"Not here," she said. "Oh, not here."

"We'll join one of the rural communities," said Henning. "We'll go at once. I'll hand in my notice, and we'll square up and go."

"And when we're there, we can start a family."

"That's it. Once we're out from under this cursed radiation blanket, we can start. We can live on the old pattern. We can live in the older traditions, as men and women were meant to live."

They kissed. It was as though they had taken a vow, and felt purified.

Myrna said: "It'll be like escaping from a plague spot into clean air."

Which showed how little they knew. Henning was a scientist of sorts, but specialisation had numbed some of his faculties. Certain concepts just did not cross his mind. He did not trouble to ask himself certain questions, let alone to seek the answers, which could so readily have been given to him by any competent authority. It did not occur to him, even for a moment, that they might already be too late.

They escaped. They ducked out from under the radiation blanket and went to live with the Southerden Community.

And they were happy, and Myrna conceived and produced a son.

That is how I come to know so much of the workings of their minds. For I am their son, whom they called Peregrine and christened in the old harbour church in the old tradition...and I entered this world with the inheritance of my parents' knowledge and memories.

At first they did not realize. Physically, I was help-less, and to them I was merely a baby—tiny, wet, hungry, demanding.

And adorable.

Later, perhaps, they would realize the irony of it. But I doubted it. I doubted whether they could ever appreciate my feelings as I lay there. Of course they were both primitive Newmen themselves, but their memories of infancy were oddly blurred. I tried, lying there in my cradle, to sort out the memories of Henning and Myrna on this topic; but I found that there was some psychological block that would not allow them to think back that far. They denied the concept of the Newmen with both consciousness and subconsciousness.

For a few months, then, I was like any other baby.

However far I might reach with my thoughts, however impatient I might be to speak and move, I could not control the appropriate mechanisms yet. When I was hungry, I had to cry like any other infant—it was the only way of attracting attention.

It was humiliating. But I could tell that it would not last for long.

Yes, I could tell. Lying in my pram outside the cottage, I would quietly practise words. It was only a matter of application. Once I had mastered the movements of mouth and lips, even the inadequacy of the childish voice was no real deterrent.

There was one man who suspected, right from the start.

This was old Clayton, the self-appointed senior member of the Community.

I remember him leaning over the pram one morning and staring down at me with his disconcerting, pale grey eyes.

There was something ruthless about him—something crude and domineering. I was frightened. There was nothing I could do to defend myself if....

Then Myrna was there, saying, "Isn't he coming on well?"

Clayton nodded slowly and sceptically.

"Looks very intelligent," he said in his rasping, unmodulated voice. "Too intelligent, if you ask me. Too intelligent by half."

Myrna laughed. Clayton went on staring at me for a moment, then turned away.

He came again. He seemed to make a point of coming to peer at me. I was sure he was waiting for me to give myself away. And I was afraid I might do so. It would be so easy; and once done, so irrevocable.

Myrna said to Henning: "That Clayton man is getting a bit queer in the head. I don't like the way he leans over Peregrine."

"He can't do any harm."

"I'm not so sure," said Myrna.

Neither was I. Clearly the time was approaching when I would have to declare myself, and Myrna and Henning, at any rate, would have to know what I was. A life of deceit was utterly impossible. To remain pent up in a child's body without being allowed the full play of the mind would be intolerable. Already I was fretting, wanting to shake off the bonds and put ideas into practice—ideas that would startle my parents and the rest of the Community, but which could not be left lying dormant.

* * * * * * *

One sunny afternoon I was put out in the pram as usual. Myrna was uprooting one or two weeds near the gate, and in the distance I could, by twisting my head and thrusting up slightly over the edge of the pram, see old Clayton on the comer of the village street. Beyond him, the masts of two of our fishing boats jutted up from under the harbour wall. He was gossiping as usual. Soon he would turn and come this way, and have a look at me. And this time he might see, and act—crudely and impulsively, as I was sure he would act in all the circumstances.

I said: "Myrna, don't go in without me."

She straightened up and looked round, startled.

"Who's that?"

I said: "Take me indoors, Myrna."

Colour fled from her face. She gave a shaky little laugh and shook her head feebly. "Oh, no," she said. "No. Oh, please, no."

"Quickly," I said. "Before Clayton comes."

She pulled the pram towards the house, and carried me indoors. She was trembling so much that I was afraid she would drop me.

When we were inside, she put me down on the couch

and stared at me as though I were a monster who had crept in from the sea—a hideous changeling.

She said: "You spoke. Out there. You...you spoke."

She wanted me to be silent. I could see that she longed to be reassured, somehow. A moment's aberration, that must be all it was. It couldn't really have happened. I had not said a word. She must have imagined it.

But there was no escape for her.

"Yes," I said. "I spoke."

Her knees gave way. She slumped into a chair.

"What shall we do?" she murmured.

"When Henning comes home," I said, "we'll discuss it."

It was an absurd relief to her. She was glad to postpone discussion. Knowing her as I did—knowing her through and through, as I knew her husband, my father—in every fibre of my being, I sensed her fatal cowardice. It was odd that she could be so forceful in some ways and so weak in others. Stubbornly, she had hated the world of the Newmen—bravely, she had faced the discomforts of exile in the Southerden Community; and yet now she wanted only to dodge the issue—to shut her ears and refuse to listen.

Of course, it must have been a shock. To have turned her back on the Newmen, to have hated so violently the idea of a child who would be master of the home, and then to find that the revolt had come too late....

Yes, I was sorry for her.

And for Henning.

* * * * * * *

His drawn face, wrinkled with salt and the sun, peered down into mine when he got home. He brought the smell of the sea into the room; and he brought the smell of fear.

I said: "There's nothing to worry about. I'm not an enemy. You must realize that. I belong here, not with those creatures in the cities."

"I don't understand," he muttered. "We left before we...before...."

"The radiations must have done their work on your genes before you left the city," I patiently explained; as though to a fumbling child. "It was an obvious possibility. It was one which you could have checked if you'd given it a moment's thought."

I tried not to sound too scornful. They ought to have known; but they were obstinate and impetuous, and they had not wanted to face up to any disagreeable possibilities.

Myrna took Henning by the arm. "We've got to keep this quiet."

"This is something you'll never keep quiet," he said.

"If anyone else finds out, we'll be turned away. The Community won't allow this. We don't know what they might do."

I said: "It can't be hushed up indefinitely. For one thing, I'm not prepared to lie low and go through a wearisome pretence of being 'educated' in the slow way that things are done here." I had a pretty good mental picture of what the primitive school here must be like. "But we can probably manage to conceal things for a couple of years while I work out my plans."

A shadow flitted across Myrna's face. "Plans?"

"There are things to be done," I said.

They both studied me with an apprehensiveness that would have been comic if it had not been so pitiful. They saw me as one of the threats from which they had fled. Already, it seemed, I was preparing to run their lives for them.

Henning put it into words. He had difficulty. There had not been time for him to adjust—his rather senti-mental affection for me as a baby could not be immedi-ately cancelled out and replaced by this new mistrust. He fumbled, and at last managed to say:

"You're...one of the Newmen."

"No more than you two are," I reasonably pointed out. "And I'm on your side."

It was a simple statement, but even so, they could not grasp it. It was no use trying to explain there and then. They were in no state to comprehend. I grew tired of them staring at me so blankly and hopelessly, and in a fit of irritation I told them to go away and let me rest.

They went. Slowly they backed out of the room, still watching me in horrified fascination. They might almost have been expecting me to get up and pursue them.

I wriggled my still unresponsive body into a more comfortable position, and then practised movements for twenty minutes. By the end of that time I could control my arms and fingers, but I knew that I was not ready for walking or anything too ambitious in the way of physical effort.

It was time for a sleep. So I slept.

Henning and Myrna did not return until I called them. The moment they reappeared, I could tell from Henning's face that they had reached some solemn decision. I could guess what it was.

Henning said: "We have decided that we must go away. Perhaps in one of the provincial cities we can fit in somewhere. Our duty to you and to the Community—"

"Please don't get mixed up in a lot of idealistic imponderables," I said. "Sit down and listen to me."

My voice was stilted and high-pitched. The inadequacy of it annoyed me. But they did not resist its authority. They sat down.

I went on: "You don't seem to realize that, although I belong technically to the strain of the Newmen, I have inherited all your dislike of their civilization. In me, your rebelliousness is doubled. In fact, I'm prepared to go a lot farther than you are."

"In what way?" demanded Henning.

"In opposing the child dictators of the city," I said. "In opposing the whole concept of the Newmen, which is an affront to the dignity of adult man."

"But how can you? It's...well, it's unnatural. We can't expect you not to behave like the rest. The way you talk...the way you are. How can you make out you're opposed to them?"

"I'm aware of the apparent contradiction," I assured him. "But it will all be resolved in good time. Time,"

I added, "is what I need. Time for thought, and planning. A year or two—during which we must keep the secret from Clayton and the others."

I refused to explain further. There was too much in need of clarification in my own mind before I would confide in others; before I could give my orders.

The Community would learn in due time. The Community would be grateful to me, eventually.

* * * * * * *

For two years I was patient. For two years I went slowly and cautiously. I made a show of learning to walk in the clumsy, old-fashioned way that was common to all the children in Southerden. I evolved a ridiculous baby speech for public use—and rarely used the adult language I knew, even to my parents, for it only upset them, and they could rarely grasp what I was talking about.

The weeks and months went by while I studied the situation and tried to shape the future to my own satisfaction.

Through the information and visual images acquired from my mother and father, I knew nearly all there was to know about the Southerden Community. There had been few new developments in the area since I had been born. When I was in any doubt, or wanted to check on a point, I asked Henning briefly for details. Reluctantly, he would answer my questions. He no longer tried to treat me as a baby—his early affection had gone now, and his face was bleak with loss. It was only with the greatest difficulty that he could bring himself to play the game in public of being an adoring father.

Myrna was better. She sometimes had a yearning expression in her eyes when she looked at me, though, did she hope that somehow it would all turn out all right?

I saw Southerden, through their eyes, as they had seen it during the first few weeks after their arrival. They had been happy then. Their vague idealism became exultant. Life was simple and full of promise.

The fishing village of Southerden stood at the entrance to a small harbour. Behind it, the hills rose gently to farmland above. The arc of the bay formed a protective arm—it enclosed the village from the wind, and the hills helped to cut it off from the world that its inhabitants had left.

Fishing and farming—two of the oldest means by which man had learned to exist on this planet. Basic and primitive.

The sea and the land, offering their eternal challenge.

Those men and women who had turned their backs on the regime of the Newmen accepted the challenge as their ancestors had accepted it. In the rhythm of village life they found satisfaction. Their children grew up gradually, and gradually learned to plough the land and draw fish from the sea. They fumbled their way towards elementary knowledge. Children here were the taught, and not the teachers.

It was deliberate retrogression. They were swimming against the tide of human progress. But there had always been such stubborn recusants, and the Newmen could afford to be tolerant.

That was one of the first essentials on which I seized. The Communities, of which Southerden was only one, owed their continued existence to the tolerance of the very people whom they most hated. If the Newmen had wished to abolish the Communities, they could have done so without effort. Only their goodwill—or, rather, their indifference—made it possible for these groups to go on existing.

We were here on sufferance.

Other folk in Southerden might take this for granted, or might never pause to consider it. But I was infuriated by the arrogance of it. To the Newmen we were all beneath contempt—we were not even worth the trouble of abolishing; we were quaint, foolish, insignificant...not to be taken seriously.

But I knew myself to be as good as the Newmen.

The seed of hatred planted in my mind by my parents germinated. Soon it would thrust up its first shoots. Soon it would blossom.

* * * * * * *

When I was old enough to be taken out for short walks without arousing the suspicion of the villagers, I often went with Myrna to the river mouth, half a mile along the coast from Southerden.

The river cut through the hills like a saw slicing through a barrier. But the river itself was the barrier.

On this side lived the Community; on the other were Newmen.

Not all the Newmen lived in towns and cities. Agriculture was still important—particularly as practised by these highly-trained, gifted experts, who tackled it with the devastating brilliance their successive generations showed in every subject. Newmen living in the country were in no way mentally retarded—prospective parents could attend mass clinics in the nearest towns and receive a modification of the original pulse injection. It was an expensive process compared with the radiation blankets of the cities; but it was nevertheless cheaper than a radiation grid system over the whole countryside would have been.

I stared across the river at farms on the slopes on the opposite side.

Smooth, silent machines clambered over the ground. Robots went gliding swiftly about their business. An occasional human being would come out to inspect the work, and would, perhaps, look across the river at us. Once a middle-aged man waved condescendingly.

Over the sea, aerial magnetic fishing went on with ruthless efficiency. Sometimes our old fishing smacks would run across the line of the aircraft, and then they would switch off and wait—again condescending, contemptuous, tolerant....

One day I was left alone in the small garden at the back of the cottage. Sunk in thought, I unlatched the gate and walked out. My steps led me down the road towards the river. I was singing to myself—a song that I knew without having ever heard it; a song my mother had known as a child.

The words shaped themselves automatically. Without realizing it, I was singing aloud, strongly.

Realization came when I found myself suddenly face to face with old Clayton. There was no time to change my expression, to look bewildered, to put on the gestures and stumbling uncertainty of a child. From the look in his rheumy eyes I knew that he saw me clearly—he saw that I was not as other children in the Community were.

* * * * * * *

I confronted them all in the Community meeting place, a wooden building on the waterfront.

At first Clayton had tried to take the law into his own hands. He had tried to have me driven away—to throw Henning, Myrna, and myself out—without any more ado. I can still hear him screaming:

"Get 'em away from here—the child-governed—they're dangerous. Out with them, before it's too late."

But I talked him down. My puny child-body quivered with an instinctive, animal fear, which I could not control, but I stood my ground and out-argued the old man. It was not too hard. I had reached far beyond his simple intelligence. I knew what thoughts and ideas to appeal to, what breaches to concentrate on in his defences. I could out-think that surly, limited mind of his.

I talked him into allowing a public hearing. It was in accordance with the traditions of the Community—the old, revered traditions. When he had agreed and gone away to arrange it, he must have been puzzled as to how he had let himself be manoeuvred into such a position.

So I sat on the platform with Henning and Myrna, and with Clayton and a couple of other older people who had founded the Southerden Community.

And I said: "My mother and father didn't want me to be a memory inheritor. It wasn't their fault. They didn't know I was going to be like this."

"But now that you are," growled Clayton, "there's no place for you here."

"I belong here."

"You can't stay."

"I not only can," I said, "I must. For your sakes more than my own. For all our sakes."

People in the body of the hall rustled and whispered. There were murmurs of mistrust.

Clayton said: "We want none of your sort here. The Communities were founded for those of us who didn't want any part in a world where children run mad."

"You've got to adjust. You've got to face certain problems. You can't—"

"We aim to keep this place the way it was when we started. Freedom from the Newmen—that's the whole idea."

"You can't just stand still," I said. "You can't allow yourselves to stagnate."

"He talks about stagnation. D'you see?" Clayton appealed to the audience, spreading his arms wide. His horny right hand clenched into a brown, knotted fist. "Like the rest of them. He wants progress, as they call it. He's here to fool us. He'll work on us—try to push us into spawning Newmen—"

"No," I said. "But the Newmen will be encroaching on us if we don't plan. Not this year, maybe, or next. But as the newer generations come along, they'll start to covet our land. They'll start to think of abolishing the reservation laws and taking us over."

"They've promised—"

"Promised! They'll find good reasons for evading their guarantees. As time goes on and their scientific progress becomes swifter, they'll be less and less patient with the scattered Communities. They'll want our land, and they'll want those of us who live on it to be out of the way. They put up with us now because the climate of opinion is in favour of tolerance. But soon...."

I went on fervently and persuasively. I hammered it into them. Naturally suspicious and resentful, they were very ready to believe in the eventual deceitfulness of the Newmen.

And they were right to believe. I knew that. The workings of the minds of the Newmen were easily comprehensible to me. The progressive temperament was something I could understand—the urge to move onwards, to lose patience with reactionaries, to pursue remorselessly that ultimate scientific perfection.

Only Clayton stood out. His pride was at stake. He refused to believe in the menace I hinted at, though if one of his own people had put it to him he would have been the most outspoken on the subject. He saw me as a usurper. There he, too, was right. In time I would take over from him. It had to be. I saw that. Already I was beginning.

He growled: "You're up to no good. I don't know what schemes you've got, but they're not good for us. You're one of them."

"In a way I am," I quickly admitted. "Enough so to know the way they think and how they're likely to act. I'm aware of their potentialities—and of my own. But remember that I've inherited from my parents an instinctive revulsion against the Newmen and all their ways."

It was difficult to put across. He would not be convinced. But after a while he grudgingly held his peace. He could not realize how irrevocably I had, in my own mind, already declared war on the Newmen.

"The day will come," I assured the Community, "when we shall restore the old order to our country. The day will come when we turn off the evil machine, and the radiation will cease to be."

* * * * * * *

I was twelve when I killed old Clayton.

I had been very busy in the intervening years. I travelled about the country visiting other Communities, inculcating the spirit of antipathy towards the Newmen and fanning the flame where it already burned. It was easy for me to get about, even to penetrate the cities— it was obvious that I was one of the Newmen, and I was allowed into the cities without protest. Adults there treated me with respect. I made my contacts. In the Communities there was widespread suspicion of the promises given by the Newmen. They were ready to listen to me. And in the cities there were surprising numbers of older people anxious for an excuse to revolt against the young folk who dominated them.

Perhaps there would always be this stratum of the disaffected. Just as younger generations in the past had broken away from their parents and defied the beliefs of their parents, nowadays the parents were resentful. As one generation succeeded another, there would always be this envy and unrest among those who felt themselves being left behind.

In some of the Communities I met one or two others like myself. Henning and Myrna had not been the only couple to delay leaving the city until it was too late. I heard stories of some who had been sent back; but there were others who had been allowed to stay. They might prove dangerous rivals. Or so I thought at first. Then, as I cautiously explored, I found that none of them constituted a serious menace. Not one had the strength of purpose that was a legacy to me from my parents. They would be my lieutenants—none of them would aspire to becoming the commander.

The organization was gradually built up. Patience was essential.

At first, as I travelled and preached the doctrine of eventual resistance to the Newmen, I was met with scepticism and suspicion. Then, as time went on, I received more and more support.

"The Newmen won't be patient for ever. The Newmen will forget their promises sooner or later. The Newmen will want our lands—and our children." That was the message I preached. Repetition drove it into the minds of the Community dwellers.

Before very long it was they who were impatient for action. They clamoured for an armed uprising. They wanted to set up sabotage groups at once, which would infiltrate into the cities and destroy the power plants.

I insisted on patience. Nothing would be achieved without long-term planning. We were puny—the Newmen were not altogether unjustified in regarding us as insignificant. When we finally struck, we had to know precisely what we were doing. There would be no second attempt if the first one failed.

I restrained the rebellious elements. A grand strategy would take years to develop. We must be sure of every man and every detail before we moved. Our contacts must be perfect, our lines of communication infallible. Surprise was everything.

The length of time involved was, I admitted, a danger in itself. In all that time, in all the quite separate groups that were held together only loosely by my travels and my growing organization, surely there would be one traitor? Word would leak out somehow.

But the years went on; the plans matured slowly;

and still the Newmen did not pounce. Nobody defected from our ranks. The mere fact that people had turned their backs on the Newmen in the first place seemed to be sufficient guarantee of their sincerity.

I moved in and out of the cities, and aroused no suspicion. I established my contacts, and none of them broke. The resistance movement took shape.

But there was still Clayton.

Old enough to be the grandfather of most of the members of the Southerden Community, he grew more and more bitter and surly as time went on. He had set himself up as the grand old man of the village, and it irked him to see me assuming control. I knew that he hated me. I knew that if ever an opportunity. presented itself, he would treat me as he wanted to treat all the other Newmen. Given an opportunity, he would have got rid of me.

Which is why I felt quite justified in doing what I did.

I had gone for an evening stroll along the shore, thinking out one or two problems of co-ordination. The rhythm of my steps kept my mind moving steadily in a similar rhythm.

Next week, I thought, I must go up north. The Newcastle group needed an encouraging word; Immured in their artificial city, they were growing restless. They wanted to overturn the children who surrounded them giving orders and wrenching life more and more out of its old pattern.

If, after that, I could go on for a few days to....

"Hello," said old Clayton.

I came out of my reverie with a start. I was annoyed. I did not like being disturbed in the middle of making plans.

I said, coolly: "Good evening."

He looked down at me and shook his head wonderingly.

Then he glanced up at the sky.

"Yes," he said. "Come to think of it, it is a good evening. Fine light on the water down there by the shore, isn't there?"

I hadn't noticed. I turned to look. Presumably he was right. But what did light on the water matter?

We were only a few yards from the edge of the riverbank, shored up here where it emerged into the sea. Beyond, lights blazed on a hillside farm, and there was a faint, gentle hum that drifted across to us.

Abruptly, Clayton said: "You'd like to be one of 'em, wouldn't you?"

"I don't know what you mean," I said—not because I didn't know, but because this was how conversation was carried on in the Communities; it caused a bad impression if I seized on a point too quickly and flashed out a comprehensive answer. Here, one did not tackle a subject directly—one nudged gently towards it.

"You'd like to be over there," he snarled, waving his hand derisively across the river. "You're one of 'em. Don't tell me different."

"You are well aware," I said, "that all my energies are devoted to planning for the day when the regime of the Newmen can be ended. I'm one of you. I disapprove of the rule of children as much as you do. It upsets the natural order of things. The balance of the human race has been seriously disturbed, and I am as determined as you are that one day it must be set right."

"So that you can be boss?"

"The question doesn't arise."

The dying sun struck a queer, fierce red spark from his eyes. He said: "Oh, yes, it does. Jealousy—that's all that drives you."

"You're mad."

"I'm not mad," he said. "I can see straight. I can see that you couldn't go back to the cities because you'd be nothing there. A nonentity. Kids of your age'd be ahead of you, and when the next lot came along you'd be one of the slaves, like every other grown man and woman in those places. So you want to rule this place instead—"

"I want to re-establish the old order," I insisted.

"And put yourself in charge? The glorious liberator, eh? The one-eyed man, king in the country of the blind...."

We stood on the edge of the bank now. I had not remembered walking there. I was conscious only of my hatred for this man—a hatred to match his own for me. Because he was old, he thought he had the right to be offensive to me. The old had many lessons to learn.

I said: "You don't understand. You never will understand."

"I understand why this Community was formed," he

said. "And I understand what will happen to it if you have your way. A war—destruction. All for your own glory. All because you're lost, son. Lost. Neither one of us nor one of them."

I thrust my face into his in the gathering dusk, and shouted: "I'm one of you. The only one with any foresight. The only one who can save you."

"Lost," he repeated. "And because you're lost, we've got to pay for it. It's a heavy price."

It was then that my patience gave out. In that instant I saw that he might still ruin everything. With his malicious tongue and his refusal to face the harsh truths of our time he might turn people against me. I could afford to run no risks. For the sake of the future—the future of the Community—action had to be taken.

So I killed him.

* * * * * *

He saw it coming, and laughed. I remember his laugh even now. I remember it in the same way as I remember experiences from my mother's and father's memories—it is etched on my mind, unforgettably, the way they are.

His eyes widened as I struck him. His harsh laugh rang in my ears for a long moment, and then fell away as he plunged from the bank. There was a splash as he struck the surface of the water.

I swayed, and then turned and went away. By the time I got back to Southerden, I had evolved a story that made the best possible use of the incident. There was no point in wasting it—it could be employed to stiffen the spirit of resistance in the Communities.

I quickened my pace as I reached the end of the village street, and looked around wildly. The first person I saw was Tom Bentley, a middle-aged man who shared one of the fishing smacks with my father.

"Hello, there, Peregrine," he said doubtfully, as I called to him.

Always they respected me, now; but always they were uneasy in my presence.

I said, breathlessly: "Something's happened along by the river. I'm sure one of our people is in trouble there."

"Who?"

"I couldn't tell. I was too far away."

"Go on." He glanced in the direction of the river. The shore was shrouded in mist, and the line of the hills above the bay was only faintly blacker than the sky behind. "What did you see?"

"Someone was standing on the bank, on our side. And he seemed to be...well, pulled in. It was as though someone in a boat had come quietly up below him. Someone...or something."

In a matter of minutes a small group was formed. Armed with knives and jagged pieces of wood, some of the burliest men in Southerden made their way towards the river. There was not a sound.

Apprehensively, the leader peered over the edge. I came up beside him.

"I'm sure it was here," I said. "One minute he was

there; the next, he was gone."

"You think someone came over and got him?"

"Someone," I repeated, "or something."

I could sense their uneasiness. The robots on the other side were hated. The uncanny, inhuman movements of those efficient creatures made the hackles rise. The thought of some deadly, remorseless, soulless thing being sent across the river for some reason, and for some reason dragging one of our own people in....

It was a nightmare. Senseless, irrational—yet compelling, like a nightmare.

"Maybe," said Tom Bentley, "it wasn't one of our folk who got pulled in. Maybe the figure you saw was one of their own people on this side."

Either way, the thought was a disturbing one. The Community wanted nothing to do with human beings from the other side, or with their inhuman creations.

We went back to Southerden. And by morning it was realized that old Clayton was missing.

He was never found. His body must have been swept out to sea by the swirling tide in the narrow estuary. That was how I imagined it; but I did not mention this to anyone. They muttered among themselves about the Newmen, who had come over and captured one of us.

"But why?" asked my father in an argument. "What point would there be in that?"

"We don't know what the Newmen are up to," said Tom Bentley darkly.

"They wouldn't want to kidnap one of us," my father persisted. "They know all about us. They know we're only men and women—we've got nothing to offer them."

"Except, perhaps, details of our plans to take back the country one day," said Tom Bentley.

The men in the small group turned to look at me.

Henning said slowly. "If your plans have involved poor old Clayton in trouble—"

"Clayton was never taken into our confidence," I returned.

And Tom Bentley at once said: "I wasn't meaning to fix any blame when I said that. It was just an idea. And if it's true, it shows that Peregrine's been right all along. If they're that sort of folk, we're right to oppose them. We're right to hit at them when we get the chance, all along the line."

They tried to discuss some way of establishing the facts of what had occurred. But it was a hopeless proposition. Where did you begin on a thing like that? The Community had, of its own free will, cut itself off from the Newmen. To appeal to the laws and judicial system of the Newmen would be to invite scorn.

"But we've got to do it," said Henning. "The laws of this country are still the laws of this country. We can send in a formal request for an enquiry. The government in London won't let Newmen in this part of the country behave just as they like. Kidnapping—murder, maybe...."

I said: "There have been deaths in other parts of the country at one time and another, and who has ever got any satisfaction from the Newmen?"

They listened to me. They had none of them made any real contact with Communities in other parts of the country, so they had only my word for these things. I told them how communications from the Communities to the Newmen were ignored, how protests were laughed at, and how impossible it was to establish even formal relations with Newmen who lived, perhaps, only a mile away over a hill or beyond an adjacent river.

"That's the way we wanted it," interposed Tom Bentley. "So I reckon we've got no grudge now. No more than we've always had, anyway," he added grimly. "Being dispossessed—grown men having to leave the cities to escape children—we've always faced up to that, and this doesn't make any difference. It only makes us more sure."

They followed his lead. They had to agree that there was nothing to be done. Nothing yet. The day would come, as I had promised.

* * * * * * *

Sometimes I lay awake and thought about what Clayton had said on that last day of his life.

It came back to me, nagging at my memory. It came back like his laugh, with a thousand echoes. Simpler people would have been able in time to blur over the words and forget them; but my mind could not relax its grip on anything like that.

"Jealousy...," he had said. "You want to rule this place instead...."

"The one-eyed man, king in the country of the

blind."

Was it true?

I came in the end to a cool recognition of my own pathological condition. This ability to analyse one's own faults was another attribute of the Newmen. I saw that the emotionalism I had inherited from my parents was driving me to behave illogically; but this realization did not in any way affect my determination. I had to accept the fact that I had certain obsessions. I knew that it was impossible to alter them. The ability to see them clearly did not mean that I could overcome them. I knew better than that. I knew better than the crude psychologists and religious moralists of earlier centuries.

Perhaps it was true that I was jealous of the Newmen who controlled the advanced civilization of the cities. I sensed what delights they experienced in the exercise of their mental faculties. My own were clamped to the ground by circumstances. In the Community I could not use my abilities to their best advantage.

But if I could not be a ruler in the cities, I would be a ruler here. I would lead a campaign.

I would be all the things Clayton had accused me of being.

And Clayton was not the only one to accuse me.

The time for action was drawing near. We had been patient, and soon this patience would be rewarded. I had chosen the time of the Conference of All Nations— when that opened in London, we would strike.

It was then that my father called me a madman.

"A fanatic," he cried in my face. "When the world is at peace, you want to make war—"

"Only on the false civilization," I said.

"It is world-wide now. As long as we are allowed to live out our lives in peace—"

"Will there be any peace in your mind if you allow the Newmen to take over the Communities? Are you going to be resigned to the dying out of the Communities? We know what we must do. And it shall be done."

World peace. That was true. But to me, and to the men who were my followers, it was a detestable peace. The boasts of the Newmen had been fulfilled; and that was an intolerable state of affairs. The spread of memory and skill inheritance throughout the world had enabled men to grapple much more intelligently with international problems—the development of an international language speedily settled many difficulties of communication, and the leaders of different countries thought and spoke on a higher plane than ever before. The World Federation was formed with a speed, which would have been incredible to politicians and pessimistic diplomats of the twentieth and early twenty-first centuries.

And the President of the World Federation was a boy of ten.

* * * * * * *

We did not have telescreens in the Communities, and we did not receive daily newscasts. The Communities had repudiated the world of dominant children, and scorned their inventions and gadgets. But in preparing the campaign I had been forced to establish some contacts within the cities, which would supply news. Important social and political information reached me by a special messenger service. We used nothing in the way of radio transmission—dealing with a world of technicians, we did not dare to use equipment that could be tapped, traced, and eavesdropped on.

I knew about the election of the President. He was Juhan Larsen, the youngest member of a family that had given a dozen distinguished scientists to the world in the last hundred years. Even before the introduction of the Newmen radiation, the name of the Larsens had been held high in world opinion. Devoted, serious, living secluded lives and working in the interest of abstract truth, they were the paragons of civilization. Little was known about their private lives—all of them kept out of the public eye. But now when a World President was needed and that man had to be of unimpeachable integrity and brilliance, it was essential that a Larsen should be drawn out into the blaze of day.

Juhan Larsen, ten years old, would open the session of the Conference of All Nations in London. Surrounded by the Federation Government who had chosen him—like a college of cardinals, I bitterly thought—he would preside over one of the greatest conclaves of representatives of nations at peace that had ever been assembled.

He would be in London; and he would die in London.

"You're a fanatic," said Henning to me yet again.

"What will the murder of a boy achieve? If the Newmen have been able to bring world peace, let us leave them alone."

"They will not leave us alone," I said. "Not much longer."

"You can't defeat them. They'll outwit you."

"No." I was sure I knew their weaknesses and knew how to defeat them. The implacable urge was not to be denied.

"What can you hope to achieve?" Henning went on desperately. "You say you're fighting against the Newmen. You claim to represent the concept of the dignity of the older generation as against the dominance of children. But you yourself have dominated the councils of the Communities. You've become one of the Newmen in thought as well as...."

He fumbled for words. He was lost in complexities with which he could not grapple.

I said: "Whatever I am, and whatever I do, it is your legacy to me."

Myrna put her face in her hands and wept. She was very emotional, and absurdly naive. And unreasonable—for it was true, was it not, that my feelings towards the Newmen were inspired by her and Henning? Because of them, I was a weapon designed to attack and demolish the Newmen. I had been fashioned only for that. In every fibre of my being I felt it.

Abruptly, from out of nowhere, a memory surged up into my mind. It was a picture of Southerden—a small village in the sunset, with a fishing boat coming into harbour.

The breeze from the sea had a salt tang, and made a faint whistling sound as it blew between the houses. I was conscious of happiness—and tranquillity.

The memory was one of Myrna's. It came from her early days in Southerden. It gave me a picture of Southerden that I rarely saw nowadays. I rarely looked at the village itself—it was merely the place in which I worked and schemed.

I felt strangely moved. This was how it ought to be. In years to come, when we had defeated the mechanistic system of the Newmen, and all people were free to live as Nature meant them to live, it would all come back to this—I would sit in my old age in a cottage, and watch the sun on the water and the children playing as children were meant to play along the shore....

It was a thought of sweet simplicity.

But I was not simple. I could never be like that. This was the ideal for which the Communities had been formed, and it was this ideal which I preached when I organized resistance to the Newmen. But for me it was not enough.

I did not yet know what would be enough.

The vision faded. I had no time for sentimentality. The road ahead was plain. It led inevitably towards the death of Julian Larsen. After that, the pattern of life would shape itself; after that, the roads would have to be built anew.

* * * * * *

On that bright, cold October day we struck.

The timing was perfect. Southern Group Five entered the power station south of the Thames and demolished the generators. There was no opposition. It was a day of festivity, and there were no guards on the power station.

In point of fact, there were no guards anywhere. The Newmen had grown overconfident, it seemed. World peace had become such a certain thing that precautions of the most obvious kind were no longer taken. The power station rocked and crumbled under the impact of carefully placed explosive. The radiation blanket over London died.

In the provincial towns and cities, similar attacks were being made simultaneously. They were equally successful.

At the same time, my forces pounced on radio stations and took over telescreen transmitters. At the very moment that President Julian Larsen was entering the Council Chamber of the World Federation Hall, erected on the site of the recently demolished Old St. Paul's, telescreens went blank for a moment. Then vision was switched on again.

All the technical details were in the hands of city-bred rebels. I had chosen carefully. I knew whom I could trust, and they did not fail. Older men who had worked for years in the radio offices all over the country now assumed control.

The Newmen had believed too firmly in their imposed peace. They were not ready for assault

"They've grown smug," I said to Michael Martin, a young man from the north whom I had chosen to act as my lieutenant in the opening campaign. "They are too complacent. They never expected a revolt from the despised country-dwellers!"

In the grand assembly, no word could reach the delegates. They were too deeply engrossed in their solemn ritual of speeches and declarations. Their faces and voices were carried out to telescreens all over the world. Even the technicians on the spot did not know that their headquarters staff had been replaced by rebels.

I watched the President on the monitor screen in Radio House, in the heart of London. It was strange to see that boy mouthing platitudes and to know that very shortly he would be dead.

In the middle of his speech of welcome, he stopped abruptly. A strange expression crossed his face. He put his right hand up to his ear as though feeling a momentary pain.

There was a murmur in the Federation Hall.

His silence lasted for a second only; but it seemed a long second. Then he looked up, and it seemed that his eyes were peering out of the screen into mine.

Something had gone wrong. But how? It was too soon for him to know yet. He had no way of knowing.

He said: "I have just received news of a misguided attack on our government. Guerrilla forces have made concerted assaults on our main cities, and seized the radio stations."

The fretful murmur in his audience rose like the roar of a descending wave, then splashed into fragments and rustled away.

"There is no cause for alarm," said Larsen glibly. "We had not prepared for such wanton outbreaks of war; but we were not altogether unprepared, if I may put it that way." His thin, confident smile was infuriating. He was talking nonsense. "Although it has been against the principles of the Newmen to maintain armed forces since the signature of the World Covenant, we have always borne in mind the possibility that unruly elements might take advantage of the new enlightenment."

Martin muttered in my ear: "Excuses, that's all."

"We have always based our policy," Larsen went on, "on the assurance that the regime of the Newmen could not be overthrown within a matter of weeks. We could have only one enemy—the reactionaries who have been allowed to live in peace away from our civilization. If these barbarians"—again he seemed to be staring into my eyes—"chose to launch an insane attack on us, we have always known that we could afford to lose a few yards."

"A few yards!" I echoed furiously.

"Things have happened as we foresaw. It is regrettable that force should once more have to be used. It is regrettable that strife should have broken out once again in a world that we believed to have been freed from the menace of war. But order will soon be restored. Already the radiation blanket, cut off momentarily by an act of sabotage, has been restored. A secondary station has come into operation—"

"Cut him off!" I snapped. "Cut transmission, and put our proclamation on."

Martin snapped an order into the internal speaker. Almost at once Larsen faded, and suddenly one of our own men was on the screen, beginning to read the message we had prepared so laboriously.

I hurried out of the room. Julian Larsen had caused a slight upset in our plans, but if we moved fast it would not be serious.

Yet how had he received that message? He could not have known before he went into the Federation Hall, for the carefully timed attacks had not been unleashed then. Nobody had approached him while we had been watching him on the screen, and he could not have received radio warning—for the radio stations were in our hands.

My commandeered helicar sprang from the roof of Radio House, and spun down like a madly windblown leaf to the landing ground by the spacious Federation Hall.

Two men moved towards me from the main door.

I tensed, then walked briskly to meet them.

One said: "Have you got a pass?"

"I'm from Radio House," I said. "Urgent news from the Controller there to the President. It's been taken over—"

"Radio House as well? We heard something from inside, but—"

"I've got to have a word with him."

If I had been an adult they might have suspected. They looked doubtful as it was; but they were in the middle thirties, and I was only a boy. I spoke in a voice of command—the tone they were accustomed to—and before they had time to wonder, or to argue, I was hastening into the Federation Hall.

The corridors were almost deserted. At one corner I saw a uniformed attendant coming out of a door. As it swung open and then shut, the murmur from the conference hall buzzed out like the sound of bees, and then was put off.

He glanced at me; but I went on, out of sight.

I knew the way. It had all been mapped out. Admittedly things were not what they ought to have been—the alarm had been given—but there was still no reason why the pieces of our plan should not lock firmly together.

Even as I opened the door of the President's ante-room, I heard the muffled thunder of the explosion outside. The sound was further away than I had expected it to be—to seal the doors, the explosion ought to have been closer and more jarring; but my men knew what they were doing.

An elderly man by the door on the far side of the ante-room turned.

"What are you doing in here? You .know the President has requested privacy. Everyone knows—"

"This is urgent," I said. "I've escaped from Radio House."

I hoped that the others were close behind me. I hoped that they were assembling by the doors of the conference hall, ready to swoop.

The man said; "He's coming off the platform now. We've heard rumours—he made an announcement...."

Julian Larsen appeared in the doorway. He was an inch shorter than I was, and I thought how insignificant and unworthy he was.

"What is it?" he asked, glancing at me.

And then his face set. Awareness blazed in his eyes.

I jumped, took him off balance, and stabbed him. Once...twice.... His head fell loosely back, and the gash across his throat began rhythmically to pour blood.

The man by the door squealed, and made a vague movement of his arm. I caught him, pulled him close, and smashed my fist into his face. He went down.

Then the door to the corridor was flung open. I swung exultantly round to greet my followers.

The faces were the faces of strangers.

Four of them were forcing me back against the wall, while another bent over the President. When he got to his feet there was a disturbing sadness in his face. No hatred, no vengeful fury; merely sadness.

He was a man in his early twenties. He came and stood before me. I thought he would strike me, but he simply shook his head.

"You have murdered a fine man," he said gently.

"That's only the beginning," I said.

"You want to spread bloodshed?"

"We want to restore the old order," I said. "I advise

you to release me at once. My men will be here any moment. We have seized power stations and radio stations. The Federation Hall, with delegates, of all nations of the world, is surrounded—"

"It is not," he said in the same gentle, weary voice.

I snapped: "My men—"

"Your men," he said, "were rounded up before they got here. Your truck of explosives was blown up at the corner of the approach."

A chill, like the first cold breeze off a freshening sea, struck me. I was alone. The men of the Communities would have to fight their way through to reach me. It might take time. They might be too late.

I thrust my face aggressively forward. "But we've got Radio House, and its subsidiaries through the country," I said. "We've destroyed power stations. You can't stop us."

"We can. We are doing so already. We are reoccupying Radio House—"

"I don't believe it."

He nodded to one of the men holding my right arm. The grip was relaxed; but still there was one man on that side with fingers of iron.

The one who had walked away thumbed a wall control, and a small telescreen blinked into life.

I looked into the face of a boy announcer—cool, reassuring, precise...and not one of my men.

Pictures began to flicker on the screen—pictures of a brief bout of fighting in the streets of Manchester; of robot labourers already dragging shattered generators away from their mountings and setting to work on the splintered flooring.

"It was a futile attempt," said the smooth-faced, sad-voiced man. "Why did you make it? Have you lost touch so completely with the Newmen that you don't understand what progress we have made?"

He was about to say something else, when suddenly he seemed to concentrate on me. I saw in his eyes the same look I had seen in those of the President

He said: "How can it be...how can you be one of us and yet not *aware*?"

"I don't know what you mean," I said sullenly.

Again he shook his head. "I see. So that is what it is? A rogue—a stray—a lost one. And you did not know that our latest two generations have developed their telepathic faculties?"

"Telepathy...!"

Of course it was to have been expected. At that level of mental development, telepathy was the next inevitable stage. And that was how Julian Larsen had received advance warning of our successful invasions of the radio stations.

"A few more generations," the unctuous voice purred on, "and we shall have no need of telescreens—or radio equipment of any kind. For the time being it is necessary for recent generations, for older people who have not been capable of developing the faculty. But soon the cumbersome equipment will be a thing of the past."

I saw the wonderful vista that could open up. It was

magnificent...but not for me.

"You did not stand a chance, did you?"

"At any rate," I triumphed, "I killed your President. That will take some explaining away."

"Your men from the Communities succeeded in the first attack because of the surprise element. Once that was over, you could not sustain your position. You yourself got in here because to older people you were clearly one of the Newmen. Again the surprise element—which could not last. Once Julian Larsen had seen you, the game was up. He sent out an instinctive warning. But we had already had a vague warning from you already—without fully realizing it, you were sending out discordant mental pulses. Many of us picked them up. We knew something must be wrong—which is why we picked up your load of explosives, and why we got to you so quickly. You yourself were the main cause of the failure of the revolt."

"You mean...I'm telepathic. I could be—"

"You could have been one of us. If you had lived with us, accepting our disciplines and our regime, you could have developed the faculty in an elementary form at any rate. But it is too late."

I drew myself up. "I did what I believed to be right," I said loudly. "And people who still believe in our cause will be heartened by the knowledge that I reached the President—that it was possible to get this close, and remove him from the face of the earth."

"The general public will never know that."

I gestured towards the crumpled body. "But—"

The door opened again. A boy came in. I looked once more into the features of Julian Larsen.

"You did not think, did you," went on that remorseless voice beside me, "that we would take chances with the President of the World Federation? He had to be the ultimate in human development—we had to elect a member of the Newmen free from errors, ideal for the post, and yet replaceable."

"It's impossible," I shouted. "There couldn't be more than one. You couldn't have an exact, identical substitute...."

None of them answered. They merely nodded towards the duplicate Larsen.

"Two of them," I said weakly.

The voice beside me said: "Identical twins. An obvious precaution, I think you will agree!"

* * * * * * *

They have given me a room with blank walls, and an unlimited supply of writing materials and a recorder, I have told them that I will dictate my memoirs, and they have agreed.

"The spirit of resistance is not dead," I have warned them. "It will never die."

They merely smile sadly, with their endless, infuriating tolerance.

"I shall dictate," I have told them, "a record of what has happened; and one day the record will be discovered, and the spark will burn again. People of the future will look back to me as the first to strike a blow against the Newmen tyranny. I shall let them see what happened. It will be an example for them."

"Yes," they gravely agree, "let them see. It will, as you say, be an example for them."

ABOUT THE AUTHOR

English writer **JOHN BURKE** was born in Rye, Sussex, but soon moved to Liverpool, where his father was a Chief Inspector of Police.

Burke became a prominent science fiction fan in the late 1930s, and with David McIlwain he jointly edited one of the earliest British fanzines, *The Satellite*, to which another close friend, Sam Youd, was a leading contributor. All three men would become well-known SF novelists after the war, writing as Jonathan Burke, Charles Eric Maine, and John Christopher, respectively.

Burke's first novel, *Swift Summer* (1949), won an Atlantic Award in Literature from the Rockefeller Foundation, and although he went on to become a popular SF and crime novelist, all his work was of a high literary standard.

During the early 1950s he wrote numerous science fiction novels that were published in hardcover as well as paperback, and his short stories appeared regularly in all of the leading SF magazines, most notably in *New Worlds* and *Authentic Science Fiction*.

In the mid-1950s he worked in publishing, first as

Production Manager for the prominent UK publisher, Museum Press, and then in an editorial capacity for the Books for Pleasure Group. In 1959 he was employed as a Public Relations Executive for Shell International Petroleum, before being appointed as European Story Editor for 20th Century-Fox Productions in 1963.

His cinematic expertise led to his being commissioned to pen dozens of bestselling novelizations of popular film and TV titles, ranging from such movies as *A Hard Day's Night*, *Privilege*, numerous Hammer Horror films, and *The Bill*. He also did adaptations of Gerry Anderson's *UFO* TV series (under his pseudonym, Robert Miall). A member of the Crime Writers' Association, he published many crime and detective novels on both sides of the Atlantic in the 1960s. He also edited the highly successsful anthology series, *Tales of Unease*.

To date he's written more than 150 books in all genres, including work in collaboration with his wife, Jean; and has also published nonfiction works on an astonishing variety of subjects, most notably music.

Now living in Scotland, Burke continues to write well into his eighth decade; in recent years many of his supernatural and macabre stories have been collected and antholologized. His latest collection, *Murder, Mystery, and Magic*, is a Borgo Press original—and Borgo will be publishing some of his classic SF and crime novels and stories in the near future.